MW00411774

Bathroom Reading

Short Stories for Short Visits

By Rick Bylina

Copyright © 2012 Rick Bylina
Published by Rick Bylilna
All rights reserved.
ISBN:1480220493
ISBN-13:9781480220492

DEDICATION

Dedicated to George and May Kalke and the double-seater outhouse at the Scott family cabin at Lake Enterprise, Wisconsin, that has saved me on numerous occasions from embarrassing situations.

Table of Contents

DEDICATION..2

Bessie 6

The Ongoing Duel..15

My Ten Minute Story Booth 21

Great Balls of Fire..27

The Kentucky Derby 30

The Effect of Tailless on the Man..................................33

Nighttime Noveling...36

The Shoelace 39

Documentaries..41

A Brighter Day 43

Shrink Wrapped..45

Writing in the Big Arena..47

A Boarish Affair...49

Mr. Jingles' Lecture...51

M&Ms on the Grass..53

True Love 55

End of Days...57

Holiday Spirit...59

Romance by the Sea...61

Shopping for Love 63

Love and the Single Girl 65

The Ant Eater 66

All's Right with the World 67

Sex..68

A True Hero 69

A Real Emergency 70

Sometimes Even Writers Get the Blues 71

Winter Lovers Torn Asunder 72

Simple Misunderstandings 73

Love on the Cuff 74

A Word Writers Never Use Anymore 75

All is Not Right with God 76

Forrest Gimp 77

Writer's Insight 78

Owe That Dog a Bone 79

Television Viewing at Night 80

The Day Timmy Found a Polar Bear 81

Fateful Decisions 82

Zombie Erotica 83

A Powerful Will 84

Death Due to Roll-on 85

First Reaction is Usually Correct 87

Sydney 88

Aaron Anderson 89

Sex and the Single Zombie 90

I Told You So 92

True Passion 94

I Don't Love PETA, But 96

Practical Gifts 98

Reversal of Fortune 100

He's no Vegan...102

Stuck in the Middle of the Middle of Everything...............104

Doctor Visit...106

The Hand Job...108

Winning Without A Conscious..110

The Pair...112

On Writing...114

The Kiss...116

Ugh!...118

The Rant to Respectability...120

Cicadacide..123

Summer Reading Program..126

On Pleasing Everybody...130

The Great Escape..134

Finding Inspiration...139

The View..144

ACKNOWLEDGEMENTS...154

ABOUT THE AUTHOR...155

ABOUT SYDNEY..156

CONNECTING WITH THE AUTHOR..............................157

~~~~~

Bessie

Bessie snorted and cleared her air passages just as the crow landed on her back. Bessie mooed; the crow cawed. It was---

"Hello. Doing okay? Nice day. Good eats. Yummy! Fat flies. Protein. Easier than worms."

The crow had been landing on Bessie at the watering hole since the middle of the hot season. Bessie just didn't want to wander around and graze on the pasture grass all day like the other cows. She moved only when she needed to. She would eat hay at the corner of the old barn, waddle to the shade of the oak tree to rest, and then tromp down to the nearby watering hole. She repeated this six or seven times a day. She'd nibble on grass either side of the path she had created, sprayed her feces as fertilizer for a new batch of grass, and allowed her hooves to break the hard ground so that seeds could gain a foothold. Every time she had her fill of water and left for the old, rickety barn, the crow would alight on her back.

This was the routine, except for milking time in the milking barn, a time she'd come to dread. The crow didn't go to the milking barn, because the man was there.

The first time the crow had landed on her back, Bessie was startled. She shook the crow off. The crow cawed several times. It was---

"How rude. What'd I do? Just hungry. A bit tired. You're big; I'm small."

The crow landed the next time with a bit more of a warning. After that, Bessie had accepted and now, looked forward to the crow's scratchy massage of her back.

Her tail couldn't reach some places any longer to shoo away the pesky flies, so the crow gobbled them like choice pieces of hay. An annoying itch remained from years ago when the man had put a yoke on her every day as part of her routine and made her walk in circles for hours, listening to the irritating sound of a grinding wheel. She hated the yoke and despised the walks in the sweltering heat or insufferable cold of the barn. That had been many hot and cold days ago. Now, the nervous crow continually changed his position, grasping her hide with his claws, scratching the unreached itch. Bessie often mooed her contentment.

She also hated the milk machine as it bled her dry and then some. The man wanted every last drop of milk she could produce. Her chaffed teats hurt all the time. The crow could do nothing about this, but Bessie had once heard a song played over and over again about two out of three ain't bad. She agreed.

So, the crow hitched a ride three to five times a day now, even as the weather cooled. Bessie didn't say much more than an occasional moo while the crow cawed incessantly. It was---

"See the hawk. Hate the hawk. Why'd the chicken cross the road? What's a road? Ha ha! No seriously, what's a road? Look Buzzards. Oh no! There's the man. Gotta go."

Whenever Bessie arrived at her spot next to the old, run-down barn, she would head-butt it, making the hay stored above tumble down. She would then wait for the mice to get some grain before she ate. Bessie hated mice and could stomp on them, but the crow was nice enough to pick them up and take them away, removing them from Bessie's sight. Life had been much better since the crow had arrived, despite the milking woes.

Today though, she didn't like the odor wafting in the wind. Bessie understood the nature of man and the cow-disappearing-into-the-smelly-building season. She knew lack of milk production was an issue. She knew it was nearing her time to disappear into the smelly building. It was routine.

She stood there thinking that she had tried her best to keep up with the fifty-five pounds of milk expected per day and dutifully walked into the milking barn morning, noon, and night for milking. It was expected routine. Cows like routine; Bessie liked routine. However, she was getting on in years. During the early hot days, she could muster only about forty pounds per day. It didn't help that the man would slap her on the backside more often now because she lagged behind in filling the tank. The slap on her leaner side just made her tense, and the flow would slow. In response, she leaked milk now and then along her path when the tension eased after milking. More than once the man said, "Your production is unacceptable." Nowadays, she was lucky she could pump out twenty pounds even with the man encouraging her to try harder.

"Stupid cow. You cost too much to feed. You'll be a side before long. Just hope I can find a buyer." Another slap on the hind quarters by the man. "Lord knows, I couldn't eat you. I should have never allowed the kids to name you. But they're out of the house. Gone to college. Settled out of state. What they don't know won't hurt them." He cackled and moved on to the next cow.

Bessie would try to explain. "Moo." The man wasn't interested in explanations. She'd ask, "Moo?" He never answered her question about what a side was. She just followed her routine.

The crow alighted per the routine after Bessie took a few mouthfuls of water. Her thirst wasn't what it used to be. She turned and headed back to the old dilapidated barn. The crow talked as usual. It was---

"Cold last night. Saw frost. Kids fledged. Life is good. Catch the Packer game last night? What's a packer? Ha ha! Moving slow today. Are you okay?"

They reached the barn; she head-butted it; mice scurried; the crow caught two. Amazing, Bessie thought.

Pop! Bessie flinched at the unusual noise. Something dropped from the sky onto the crow. He dropped the mice. Bessie backed up a few feet. The man came running. The crow flopped around on the ground in a net. It was---

"What's this mess? How do I get out? I don't like this. Where are my mice? Oh no! There's the man. Gotta go. Can't! Help! What is this?"

"Gotcha." The man exclaimed. "You black-devil, corn-stealing thief of a bird."

Bessie watched the man save the crow from the net's embrace. He put a bag over the crow's head. It didn't calm the crow. He cursed the man and called out a word of caution to the other crows gathering nearby. It was---

"Fly away. Save yourselves. Fly away."

Bessie listened. She realized that the multiple voices from the gathering crows were his family: father and mother, grandparents, cousins, aunts and uncles, and three of his kids, about twenty altogether,

9

though Bessie wasn't very good at math. They were all screaming for the man to let the crow go. Bessie chewed her cud, confused. This was not the routine. The crow scratched the man several times, and before the man put the bag over the crow's head, the crow had bitten him twice. Feisty. Bessie had heard the man call the old gray mare that once. It fit. The man carried the crow to the smelly building, and Bessie wondered if the crow was going to become a side. Whatever that was.

Later the man came back outside. He had tied a dried corn cob with the husk pulled down over the end to a small bit of twine. He had tied the other end to the crow's feet. Was the farmer giving the crows something to eat?

The farmer lifted the crow, displaying him to the other crows who'd become silent. "Y'all get your noisy, crop stealing selves out of here or one by one I'll do the same to all of you. I know your routine."

The man pulled out a small stick. It was a special stick. Bessie had seen it before and didn't like it. The man used it to make fire for the other smoky thing he put in his mouth. Bessie was very much afraid of fire. She stomped the ground and backed up a few more feet. She was glad the other cows were out in the big field. Fire had made them run stupid in the past, and she didn't feel like running, but she didn't want to be near the other cows or the fire. It was hot, it hurt, it smelled, it made other things burn. And then there would be more fire, and the other cows would run. And she couldn't run fast any more. She did not want to die in a stampede. That would be stupid. It wasn't the routine.

Bessie looked on, captivated by the scene. The

man whipped the bag off the crow's head, and then lit the stick. The stick lit the husk on fire. "Here take this back to your nest." He let the crow go with the husk on fire. Flames licked toward the crow's backside. The crow flew. The farmer laughed. "Burn, baby, burn." The crow screamed his caws. The other crows screamed back. "What do we do? What do we do?" The crow could barely fly, but he rose, flames tickling his tail feathers. The effort seemed difficult. He screamed his caw. It was---

"It hurts! It hurts! Damn, it hurts!"

He flew to the farmer's house and barely reaching the roof. The farmer stopped laughing. He ran at the crow. "Get the hell off my roof." He picked up a rock and threw it at the crow. The crow obliged and started flying again. He was screaming louder. The other crows were screaming. Bessie was mooing, shedding great big tears to the ground, because she knew fire was hot and hurt. She knew this was wrong, but didn't know what she could or should do about ending the commotion.

The exhausted crow paused on the smelly building before the farmer threw rocks at him again. He flew off the smelly building after a small rock nicked him. The farmer turned and looked at his house. The burning husk of the cob had caught the roof on fire. The man ran to fetch the hose. The crow landed on the milking barn with a thud. He cawed. It was-

"Help me. Help me. I'm dying. I'm dying."

Bessie mooed long and mournfully. The crow glided down, plopping on the ground in front of her. The first of the crow's long tail feathers had caught fire, the nasty singed smell reached Bessie's nostrils.

She wrinkled her nose, and then stepped forward and sniffed the crow. Smoked filled her nose. The fire flickered at her snout. She snorted, and for a moment, the fire retreated. Bessie snorted again with all her might, emptying her massive nasal passages. The fire backed away momentarily. Despite the pain of the fire's return brushing up against her chin, she chewed through the twine. She brushed the freed crow away from the flaming cob with her singed snout. The crow had just enough strength to flap up onto her back.

With crow aboard, digging his claws into her hide, she ran to the watering hole.

Memories of being a calf, running endlessly against the wind and flopping without a care into the water erupted. The man's young ones ran with her and leapt into the water beside her. Her time spent during those first hot days, trying to float like a duck, despite the bad moos from the other cows. Days when the kids climbed over her, and she gently shook and bucked them like her dad did to other big men. Long forgotten feelings arose from those days before milking and walking in circles and milking and slapping and yelling came into her life as her routine. She had been happy and joyful.

She barreled into the cool water. The crow fell in with her. She stuck her whole head beneath the surface.

When she came up for air, the pain had lessened. The crow, with wings outstretched, floated on the surface like a strange black duck. He cawed in relief; she mooed a laugh. Ducks always made her laugh. The other crows had gathered around and were all cawing so loudly and at the same time that Bessie couldn't understand what they were saying. Then, at once, they grew silent. The crow farted in the water; all the crows guffawed their caws. Bessie mooed.

A scream erupted behind her, and Bessie turned around to see the milking barn glowing bright yellow and red from the flames. Smoke filled the air. The man was spraying his hose everywhere, but all the buildings were burning, except the dilapidated barn where Bessie's hay was stored.

Hours later, Bessie lay under the oak tree, exhausted. The crow sat on her back, still and quiet. The rest of the crow family had gone back to their nests. Many other men had come and gone. The house, the smelly building, and the barn were black, smoldering heaps on the ground. Bessie's barn mates had been moved to other fields or neighboring barns. They had to be milked. It was routine. Bessie would sleep under the oak tree tonight. The man in the white coat felt that was best.

"Take some time to rest old gal," he had said.

When Bessie lay down, several pounds of milk had squeezed out of her and pooled in a low spot. Mice and a barn cat from the milking barn had called a truce and lapped up the milk. The spillage was enough to make Bessie feel comfortable. The man in the white coat had gently rubbed something on her snout, chin, and cheek. It had made her face feel better, and she had allowed the crow to wipe the tips of his burnt tail feathers in the greasy ointment. It seemed to make him happy.

The light was fading; the wind had changed direction and a gentle cool breeze replaced the acrid smell. A big moon rose in the sky. She hoped she'd have the dream where she jumped the moon. It was such a pleasant dream. In the dream she was weightless and without a care.

Over by the milking barn, the man was sobbing. Bessie felt sorry for him. A man in blue stood next to him, writing something down on a piece of paper. "Just how much corn could that crow have been stealing?" The man shrugged his shoulder, shook his head, and sobbed harder.

The crow cawed once: It was---

"Thanks." He bent his head backwards into his folded wings and was sound asleep in moments.

Bessie sighed a deep long moo. She thought about the weird day. She was so tired. More tired than she'd ever been in the twenty-three times she'd seen the hot day seasons and cold day seasons. The man's actions hadn't been part of the routine, and she wondered what it all meant. Bessie didn't have deep thoughts. She was just a cow and glad the fire hadn't done any real damage. The other cows were milked and safe; the crow lived; the man was still there to fix the routine. She chewed her cud a few times, snorted, and then went to sleep for the last time.

~~~~~

The Ongoing Duel

I ran out of words the other day, so I headed to the liquor store to buy some inspiration. On the return trip, I bumped into a new acquaintance, Ralphie.

We exchanged greetings and chatted about nothing in particular. I gave him one of my beers, and then lamented, "I'm all out of words."

"Try vociferous." His flat voice reflected what seemed to be his lack of interest in my dilemma.

"Generous," I said and laughed on my walk back home at his singular word of encouragement. I sat down at the typewriter, eschewing my computer. The mashing sound of the keys always made me feel like my first cuts at a story had substance the way I imagined true fiction writing must have felt to Hemingway or Steinbeck or any of my predecessors. I typed vociferous on a clean sheet of paper, hoping for magic. Nothing happened. That night, I went to bed feeling bereft of talent, somewhat drunk, and definitely cheated.

I saw Ralphie the next day at the same place.

"Vociferous didn't do a thing for me."

He shrugged. "Not every word can be a winner." He flicked his cigarette to the curb before leaning back against the brick exterior of a building an arsonist gutted last year, a conflagration of awe-inspiring proportions that caused me to write several unfinished stories. "Tell you what. I'm gonna give you another word for free."

I grinned at his offer, as if Ralphie had cornered the market on words. "Free. Sure. Why not?"

15

"Vapid."

"Vapid?"

"Vapid. Yeah. I didn't know you was hard of hearing." He laughed at his witticism, and then promptly shrugged, his signature move that amounted to nothing except to display his apparent disinterest in my writing problem and a lightly held belief in my need for a hearing test.

"Fine." Nothing else to say, I left.

Footsteps trailed me as I went around a corner. It's not a great neighborhood, but the rent was cheap. It had a lot of color, characters, and material for the inner city stories I was trying to write that moved me out of and beyond my natural environment; however, at that moment, I wanted to be back on Apple Tree Lane, far away from the footfalls catching up to me. I walked faster. Whoever followed seemed to pick up the pace. Satchel Paige's quote haunted me. "Don't look back. Something might be gaining on you." I took his advice and kept on moving forward. I was almost home. Before I reached the stoop in front of my building, someone grabbed my arm.

Fight or flight took over. I jerked my arm free and prepared for a struggle, a beat-down, or a mugging by striking a traditional and wholly ineffective boxer's stance. A pert blond-haired girl dressed like a guy on casual Friday stood there. "How well do you know Ralphie?" she said curtly, ignoring my pugilistic pose.

"Not well." It came out sounding like a question.

She stepped closer. "Rapacious." Her palm smacked my forehead before I could react, not that I'd ever hit a girl. She walked back the same way she had come. Stunned, the only thing I could do before she turned the corner was admire her derriere. It was perfect.

That evening, vapid joined vociferous on the shockingly white and nearly empty paper. I stared at it for hours, trying to join the words together, but my mind drifted back to Blondie and her simple question to me that felt more like a warning. The unobtainable fruit of her personage worked on my loins throughout the night. In the morning, it seemed clear that another trip to Ralphie might help. I had a hunger for Blondie that was not in keeping with her antagonistic and mysterious ways. Or, maybe it was her ways, and her ass, that intrigued me. She knew Ralphie, so Ralphie might know her.

Shortly after noon, I found Ralphie in his usual spot, leaning up against the burned out building. If he worked, I didn't know where or when. Right now, I didn't care. Blondie's question was right on. I didn't know Ralphie well. His orbit and mine intersected not more than a half-dozen times through mutual acquaintances over the past two weeks. Each time he seemed to know more about me and what I did for a living. However, his life was unwritten fiction to me.

"Ralphie. Do you know some pert blond who dresses like a guy, tight ass...." His stone-faced look stopped me cold. Smoke from his last pull on a Marlboro leaked out of his mouth and nostrils the way the building behind him smoldered through openings after the fire. The haze hung about his head like some ghastly vapors.

"That broad been bugging you?"

I swallowed and chose my words carefully. "No. Not really. Do you know her?"

He searched his pockets, lit a blunt he pulled out,

and then offered me a drag. Things being what they were, I took a hit. I coughed, losing most of my efforts, and handed it back to him. It was strong, or maybe it was because I hadn't toked on a joint in years. Booze got me drunk, and I did some decent writing worthy of a strong edit after the hangover. All that marijuana ever did for me was make me hungry and help generate non-creative sophomoric crap like "God is dog spelled backwards. Think of the possibilities." Dope never revealed any writing truths to me the way a good six-pack or fifth of Jack Daniels did.

It had been a full five minutes of nothing. Ralphie puffed and the two of us watched a handful of junker cars pass by. While looking out into the nothingness that surrounded the shell of the city that had once been something proud, he said, "I know her." I waited. "I'll give you one more word. Commensal." I pulled out my pad and wrote it down. He stared at me with a look akin to a death threat, flicking the ashes from the roach in my direction. "Stay away from the blond."

"Yeah and thanks." I needed a drink, not for writing purposes, but for courage. Barney's, a bar with no class, three pool tables, and in the evening, the world's oldest pole dancer, was only three blocks away. I had barely finished taking the first slug of my beer when Blondie, dressed in a dark, tailored women's suit, sat down next to me. Her appearance made me sit up and take notice on many levels. In her power suit, she oozed self-confidence. Her trim figure shouted sex appeal. When she spoke, her pouty lips formed words that fired up lust in my soul, not to mention other body parts.

"Whiskey," she said to the bartender then slapped me with solid intent on the cheek.

"What is it with you?" I asked, rubbing my cheek. She was under my skin now, and she knew it. But Ralphie's warning sprinted through my head. Maybe she's his sister, and she's playing a twisted game with me. I was about to confront her further, but she cut me short.

"What word did Ralphie give you today?"

"How did you know he gave me a word?"

She downed her shot. "You're an open book with blank pages, and I know his game."

"What the heck does that mean?"

"Am I wrong?" She squeezed my knee, and an electric charge ran through my body.

"Commensal," I squeezed out, feeling compelled to tell her.

"Good word. Not great, but good." She released her hand.

Now, I was beyond intrigued. "How do you know Ralphie? He didn't seem pleased when I mentioned you to him."

I swear she blushed. "So you asked about me."

Now it was my turn to blush. She leaned over and whispered in my ear. "Take me back to your place, and maybe I'll tell you all about Ralphie-boy."

It's a proven fact that a man thinks about sex once every seventeen seconds. So by then, I'd thought about her and me and carnal knowledge nine times already while sitting in the dingy light of Barney's. I wasn't going to think about sex a tenth time without me and her being outside and moving in the direction of my apartment.

Her name was Victoria, and she had known

Ralphie his entire existence. She relished being a pain in his side; he was the competition. Competition for what, I never found out before we sweated up the sheets for the rest of the afternoon. She knew plenty about me, thanks to my blabber mouthing, but she was little more than Victoria from around the area to me who had some kind of issue with Ralphie.

"I have an evening appointment," she said, throwing her clothes back on and ripping off a piece of Italian bread.

I tried not to look crestfallen. I failed.

"Ah, poor baby," she said before we kissed at the door. "Chalet," she said, pulling the door shut. Like a dream, she was gone.

Exhausted and naked, I sat down at the typewriter. The same piece of paper stared back at me. Vociferous and vapid stood out on the page, naked and alone. I typed "c" for commensal, then hesitated, then hit "h" and continued until chalet stared back at me. A cool evening breeze blew over me, and I shivered as though I were deathly cold in some far off mountains.

I hit the carriage return and typed: After I killed Ralphie, I fled. The old mountain chalet became home and the winter's howling winds reminded me of what Victoria did to save me.

I stopped typing and a story filled my head with crystalline visions. The afterglow of the day burst through my window and everything became clear; I had to make myself worthy of my muse's attentions again.

~~~~~

My Ten Minute Story Booth

I have a ten minute story booth set up in the local indoor mall. At it, customers can give me an event or an item in their lives, and then I riff a story about it. One day, a chubby, middle-aged man approached my booth with his brown-haired daughter, maybe ten, in tow.

"My grandma had this frying pan." He choked on his words while struggling with his bag. The girl looked at me, peering around the man's bulk.

"Wait. Wait. I'm feeling it. Hold on." The story came in a flash; my fingers flew over the keyboard.

#

As long as I could remember, Grandma DuBois' cast iron skillet hung on the side of the cabinet near the back door to our cabin. That is, when it wasn't being used for cooking, which was pret much every meal of every day. The cabin had one big room and two bedrooms. In the big room were the kitchen, dining area, and living room. That was the center of the cabin. We called it the main room. The wood stove was on one side of the back door; the cooking stove on the other side. Made it real convenient when wood was hauled inside during the winter. Besides, Grandma was none too keen on the idea of dirt being tracked 'tcross the floor.

"You trackin' dirt?" she yelled about hundred times a day.

Ma and Pa had the bedroom at one end of the cabin. Grandma had a six by nine section closed off by a curtain from the main room.

"Why'd I need a bedroom? I ain't popping out no more babies."

Grandpa died about the time I was born, so I guess she was correct. Me and Bobby shared a bunk bed on one side of the other bedroom at the other end of the cabin. My three sisters, Winnie, Minnie, and Bobbette were in a triple-decker on the other side of curtain in the same bedroom. Bobby and Bobbette were twins, 7, Minnie was 9, Winnie was taller than me at 12. I'm Tom. I was fourteen, but I remember the skillet incident like it happened yesterday.

Like I said, Grandma cooked all the meals in that skillet: eggs, bacon, and potatoes in the morning; slabs of ham for lunch sandwiches; and pork chops in the evening for supper, one apiece, two apiece for daddy and me, because we did most of the heavy work, and-
--

"He's a growing boy." Grandma said it once a day.

We farmed, raised lots of pigs, had some cotton, and because we faced the south side of the hill down to the creek below, we did all right. The south side is bestest for growing stuff.

Minnie and me read all the time. Grandma read a lot, too, but the only book she read was the Bible.

"Has everything in it a body needs to know," she'd say.

Grandma seemed ancient to me, but now I know better. Mama had me when she was 18; Grandma had her when she was 18. So Grandma was only 50 when the skillet incident happened, but she always seemed older.

All Winnie wanted was to be a mama, which

22

happened a lot sooner than Ma would have liked it, but Billy was a nice boy.

"Emphasis on the boy," was all daddy said the day they married.

Daddy was a bit tipsy being it was one of the few occasions for which Grandma allowed liquor in the house. Winnie was 15; Billy was 17; baby Eaphus was three months along. Winnie got her own skillet that day. She cried. I told Billy that he needed to learn to duck.

Bobby and Bobbette whined a lot. The double B's were both busy being the babies in the house, they each felt like they never received enough attention. I thought it was funny when they both decided to run away. Pa found them a block apart down in the city. Not a lick of brains between them. They'd ran away without money or a plan or their rain slickers. Both caught pneumonia. Swear they just wanted to see which one of them could make everyone else the most miserableist. They did a good job most of their lives.

Well, it was a fine autumn day in late October. Rain and sun had been good all summer.

"In proper proportions," Grandma said.

Dinner was over, the sun down, but the darkness was not full. Minnie and I were reading by twin candles in a corner of the big room. Grandma and Ma were washing dishes in the washtub. Winnie was quilting a spread. Pa had cleaned his hunting rifle and now was pretending to read the newspaper. The double B's were doing their school lessons in another corner of the room. Grandma was wiping down the skillet (you never dunked it in water), and my mom was bringing the tub of water to the door to throw in the ditch outside. It was water, but the mosquitoes hated the scented soap Grandma made so it was like mosquito repellent next to the door.

Well, Ma opened the door, and a big fat black bear, some 600 pounds of mean, was standing there. She screamed. The bear screamed. The double B's screamed. Pa fell backward out of his chair. Winnie hid under her quilting spread. Ma threw the water on the bear. He got mad. Ma ran to her bedroom as the bear entered the cabin. Minnie threw her book at him. I guess he didn't like Beatrix Potter cause he tore it up on the spot. I went for the gun behind me up on the wall, but Pa had not put back in a round after cleaning it. I could see his suspenders were tangled up in the rocker, and he was flopping on the floor, eyes wide as a hoot owl coming in for a fat mouse.

Well, that bear fixed his eyes on me, and all I could do was growl at him while the double B's continued to scream. Just then, Grandma smacked that bear in the nose so hard that I swear to this day I heard the bones crack in his head. He flopped down right there on the floor.

"Well, get to skinning, looks like some good lard on that bear for pies," Grandma said.

The iron skillet was never the same. The dead center collected grease, but that's were the best tasting food was always saved for the special person of the day, according to Grandma. Though the house has changed a lot since then, I still live there with my wife. Raised three kids there. Got me six grandkids that come by on weekends.

Grandma made it to 100, cooking in the skillet all the way up to the end. The side cracked the day after her funeral, but it's still hanging on the side of the cabinets by the back door. Never know when it might be needed again.

#

I printed the story and handed it to the man. He smiled sheepishly, but didn't go for his wallet. He reached into one of his bags as he spoke. "Uh, I thought you were the information booth. Could you tell me where I can buy another pan like this?" He pulled out a Calphalon frying pan.

Glad I wasn't writing a novel. Would he have stood there until I finished *War and Peace*? "*Bed Bath and Beyond*," I said, pointing toward the other end of the mall.

He left, pulling his daughter along with him.

I wrote two more stories in the next hour. It was a good evening overall. I made $30, but after the frying pan story, my inspiration wasn't hitting on all cylinders.

I closed early. My booth collapses in about five minutes and fits nicely on a hand cart that doubles as my computer table. I slung the computer case over my shoulder and headed for the exit. I listen to the sounds of the mall behind me when I leave. I try to imagine new stories about the people based on just their footfalls. There's shuffling man, looking for presents for his grandkids. Next, I focus on the hard-as-nails, staccato tick-tick-tick of an anal-retentive woman executive as she charges across the tile. She has entered fifteen minutes in her day planner to find her spouse's birthday gift. There's the floppy sound of small feet running to catch up with the family after spending too much time gazing at bunny rabbits in the pet store.

I reach the door just as the floppy footsteps come up behind me.

"Mister," she says breathless.

I turn around. It's the little girl who had been with the pan man. Her face is a mixture of glee and concern.

I slap on a smile. "Hi there. Did you get a new frying pan?" My concern is genuine for her sake.

"You made my daddy cry."

I'm surprised and taken aback. "What?" I couldn't possibly imagine what I could have done to do such a thing. "I'm sorry. Is he okay?"

"He's fine now." She thrusts an envelope toward me. "He told me to give you this to you."

I took it. I watched as she ran away. At a corner, she met up with her daddy. They waved goodbye and walked away. I figured there had to be ten bucks in there, my going rate, maybe $20 since I'd made him cry after walking away without paying.

I ripped it open and was stunned. Six crisp $100 bills and a note were inside.

Great story. Grandma would have loved it. She passed this weekend. Never underestimate the power of the imagination to drive the written word.--Tom Dubois.

~~~~~

Great Balls of Fire

Barbara, a professional bowler, on her one and only excursion to Leroy's Nudist Beach on a dare with her best friend, Nanette, tripped over Bob.

Despite Bob's lagging personal endowments, she accepted his invitation for a beer at the local bowling alley. There, she rolled a 289 to his 187. Humiliated in front of his friends, they argued. She left.

He begged forgiveness the next day. "I never met a woman with such integrity." She forgave him and suggested paragliding along the shores of Lake Michigan. He rose four feet off the ground, but the wind slackened and he crashed like a duck shot in a fall hunt. He broke his leg.

She comforted him, helped him regain his health, and realized, while doing his *Meals On Wheels* route, what a nice guy he really was. But then, Larry, a former bowling pairs partner paraded proudly like a peacock back into her life, suggesting one more run to the nationals. She resisted. Bob needed her.

"I need you," Larry confessed. "You weren't only my partner, but I love you," Larry's tears dripped onto her hands.

Unaware of Larry's personal confession, Bob encouraged her to go. She went.

Larry and Barbara blew through the quarterfinals, and then needed a turkey in the tenth frame by Barbara in the semi-finals to reach the finals. He begged her for a romantic dinner the night before the finals. She melted to his smooth talking ways. That night, Larry pressed her hard for romance. She caved.

After Larry left her room, she washed up in the

27

bathroom. She had the television on to hide her gentle sobbing over her betrayal of Bob. It switched over to *Cheaters*, a show about cheating spouses, boyfriends, and girlfriends, where they are showcased being unfaithful. To her shock, the summer rerun showed Larry toying with the affections of the married woman of one of his significant sponsors. He was a player with no remorse.

Ashamed, she left for the airport where Bob had just arrived on the plane she needed to board to leave. She ran to him; he limped to her.

#

Sunday afternoon at the lanes, Larry sweated before the cameras. If Barbara didn't show in one more minute, they would forfeit the match to the 4Ds, Darryl and Darleen Darylrimple-Dorchestershire, the first amateur team to ever advance to the finals.

Barbara parted the doors. Larry smiled for the camera and saved his fuming words for her on the lanes. "Where were you?"

She ignored him and bowled. Larry bowled as if he had never seen a bowling ball. Barbara crushed the pins with a 300 in the first game. Still they led the 4Ds by only ten points. In the second game, Barbara threw another 300. Larry fouled twice, dropped his ball behind him, and bowled only a 134. He overheard an announcer analyze his game as "pathetic." Larry shriveled inside. The 4Ds led by twenty going into the third and final game.

Barbara continued her string of perfection; Larry rolled better. 4Ds continued with their own brand of consistency. Barbara was the anchor and by her turn in the tenth frame as the last bowler, she needed only two strikes and two pins to win. She was in her groove and nailed the first two strikes.

"This is history being made," the announcer whispered into the microphone loud enough for everyone to hear. "No one has ever bowled a perfect series in competition."

Larry slapped a high-five with a blond spectator, sporting a too-tight tube top. He mocked the 4Ds as Dumb and Dumber, and Dumbest and Dumdum.

Barbara picked up her ball, and then turned to the crowd. Ignoring the camera and focusing on Bob, she said, "I retire after this ball."

The crowd roared in appreciation of her long career and spectacular game that day. She faced the pins, and began her approach.

Next week, Barbara accompanied Bob to Leroy's Nudist Beach as man and wife. A buxom woman approached them shortly after they lay their blanket.

"Aren't you the pro bowler?"

"Retired pro bowler," Barbara corrected.

"Yeah. What you did took balls. I thought that ahole partner of yours would have a stroke when you laid down that perfect gutter ball.

"Who says I did it on purpose?" Barbara smiled, tugging Bob toward the water.

"Nice flag pole," yelled the woman on the shore to Bob.

Bob smiled. Barbara glowed, admiring Bob's….

The Kentucky Derby

Last night I dreamt I went to Louisville again.

Horses ran in the Kentucky Derby, and then feasted on flowers adorning the hats of privileged women ogling for the cameras in the winner's circle as if they had anything to do with a thousand-pound athlete, straining against exhaustion in a two-minute sprint with a childlike man on their back, showing the accursed whip from time to time.

Real horses need no whip. Secretariat didn't need a whip. Real horses run because that is their fun, flinging dirt clogs into the eyes of the other equine, spraying foamy sweat. The measured breath of a fine-tuned force of nature beating a cadence that shuts out the screaming of over 100,000 humans was their joy.

The winner ate roses; the losers ate dandelions, yellowing their large teeth that were bleached white the night before for their promised close-ups. These horses seemed betrayed, ashamed, but only one can win. One can almost hear them snort, "I did my best. I didn't run this hard so I could be beaten."

My heart raced along with the fastest two minutes in sport, and it woke me.

I sat up in bed, waiting for my racing heart to slow to a slow canter. I reached over and put on the hat for a lark. I smiled and remember the first time I went to Louisville.

Two bridges were out. Heat rose from the road approaching town. Cars clogged the remaining highway like cholesterol in a fat man's arteries while eating a deep-fried doughnut wrapped in bacon at the state fair. The snarled traffic caused drivers to beat

30

their horns like deranged drummers. I exited the highway onto a side road.

When a mounted cop stopped next to me at a traffic light, his horse defecated, and then blew snot on my windshield in derision at my caged horses. The cop laughed. I'm not even sure he was from Louisville. Something else was going on, but I hadn't a clue.

A number of people on horseback crossed in front of me. Some invisible trigger caused them to break into a fast trot up the street. I went the other way, and I lost them as I drove on. Like a fish caught in a seine, I was enveloped by cars once again. I surrendered to the in inevitable truth that I was going nowhere fast and parked my car.

A solid stream of country music came from the corner tavern. I drank, and later, to the tune of "My Old Kentucky Home" I drank a disgusting drink called a Mint Julep.

In the haze of good buzz, I watched the horses come down the home stretch on a fuzzy television mounted too high. A large red blur roared to the finish like a mighty engine just beginning to power up. The place went nuts. Some brown-haired girl in a broad-brimmed hat decked out with daisies, more sloppily drunk than myself, kissed me. She kissed me long and hard, and soon our tongues battled for dominance.

We came up for air. "Nice," she said. As her blood-shot brown eyes closed again, she mumbled, "Great derby." She was almost passed out and now, by default, she was my responsibility. I accepted the task and helped her to her apartment.

It was a PG affair. I was drunk, not a moron or a

pig. I covered her with a quilt; she rolled over. "Thanks." A minute later, she was snoring. I drifted off to a drunk's deep sleep for two hours, woke, and drank the last of her stale coffee. I left my number, knowing she'd never call, and that I'd return someday to find her divorced with two kids, working at the bar, and having no memory of tonight.

All of Louisville slumbered as I drove, being trailed by a full moon. The night was more twilight eve at four in the morning than anything else. The bridge appeared two miles and two minutes ahead. The local radio station cued up the play-by-play call of the derby one last time. "They're off!"

That night, I put on the souvenir hat from the girl, hit the gas, and showed my horses the whip.

~~~~~

The Effect of Tailless on the Man

A glob of PB&J plopped onto my walkway as I sat on my front steps. Firefighters scrambled back and forth into my neighbor's house. I was too tired to get up and see what the problem was. I should have pretended concern. He was my neighbor after all, but he was nuttier than the squirrel in front of me.

The fat, tailless squirrel had been around for months. He was a real nuisance, emptying bird feeders, trying to bolt past me into the house, and even banging on the sliding door when I ate. He sat five feet in front of me and stared in my direction like a pathetic orphan wanting more. The look lasted for ten or fifteen seconds, which is a lifetime for a squirrel.

Begging was part of his routine to get sweet treats. Next, he ran to the baby camellia bush and leapt at it like a lion onto a hapless gazelle. Then he started the process all over again. Perhaps he was just trying to demonstrate how fearless he was. Even the occasional shadow from a circling redheaded turkey vulture overhead did not seem to faze him. I glanced up and watched the lazy looping pattern of the vulture. Something must have died nearby, but my summer cold had rendered my sniffer useless. I smelled nothing.

"No leftovers, you bum. I have to survive on too little as it is." He didn't seem to care about my problems.

Ten minutes later, the firefighters were through with the emergency at my neighbor's house.

"Small electrical fire," one said, returning to his

truck and carrying an empty fire extinguisher that he casually lifted into the hopper.

"What caused it?" the rotund cop asked. He remained leaning against his car while controlling the crowd of six elderly neighbors, two kids straddling their bikes, and the young couple who had moved in down the street.

"Looks like something chewed on an electrical line in the attic."

My neighbor, ever a gracious bastard, trailed the fire chief across the lawn.

"You didn't have to trample my pansies. Why didn't you use the sidewalk? Who fixes the damage in my attic? Do you guys clean it up?" The chief responded, "No time, you, and no."

I chuckled.

The chief climbed into the cab of the truck. The engine started. The mass hordes dispersed while my neighbor returned to his house, grumbling all the way. The fat cop rolled out of the intersection in his patrol car, which squeaked its need for a new pair of shocks. The main event was over.

I threw Tailless a leftover crust coated with a thin layer of guilt and a sprinkling of revenge. "Bon appetit. May your teeth rot."

He ran into the street and squatted in the shade of the fire truck with his prize. The truck moved. Startled, Tailless dropped his supper and then chattered angrily. He darted left, right, left, and then sprang at the tire with a kamikaze scream. I think Tailless bit the tire before it rolled over him.

Conflicting emotions overcame me, as he became dinner for a hungry vulture, which swooped down long before you would have expected one to descend on the recently deceased.

I retired inside to Jerry Springer. Where does he get those pathetic people? Tailless would never entertain me again, but he would also never chew on the wires in my house as he had probably done to my neighbor. The satisfied grin from saving my house from my neighbor's fate morphed into a confused frown over what I've lost from the fringes of my shrinking life.

~ ~ ~ ~ ~

Nighttime Noveling

At four in the morning, it is very dark. Deer roam with their big eyes and sensitive noses finding my landscaping *magically delicious* and eating until they're too fat to run away from cars on the highways. Raccoons dig like British soldiers in German POW camps, silent and effective, uprooting more often than not, my most prized bushes. Thank God the squirrels sleep at night, but the neighborhood dogs bark at coyotes traipsing on the edge of man's domain. Do rabbits dream of green grass? Have all the snakes slithered into their hidey holes? Why do owls have such noisy sex? They sound like a band of monkeys fighting over a *Fig Newton*. Distractive thoughts stir at every turn.

Sixty-six degrees in mid-November is unnatural, and so is having the window open. *Frosted Flakes* taste good in the morning. I used to eat *Sugar Pops*, which now sports a more politically correct name, *Corn Pops*. However, they contain stuff used for embalming people. Yuck! I'm sure it's an urban legend.

The newspaperwoman drives in like a *NASCAR* wannabe and drops the *News and Disturber* at the end of my neighbor's driveway. I'm sure she flips me the bird as she drives away. I cut the last of the paper umbilical cord a month ago, and I've noticed tire tracks appearing mysteriously on the edges of my roadside lawn.

I have 28,000 more words to kill, and most hide in the dictionary, quivering, concerned about their fate. The strong nouns and vibrant verbs don't care. They lean against the edge of the pages, aloof. They know they'll be the first to go. They'll fling themselves at the strongest construction without care, building a foundation for the words that follow their lead.

Two hours later, my wife stirs. My sugar mama readies herself for work.

"Tea?" She suggests.

"Bourbon." I counter.

She scurries away. I hear her failed attempt at a Bronx cheer, a bilabial fricative is what I think George Carlin called it, may some deity rest his soul.

Arnie the Armadillo smiles from atop the computer. He can afford to be smug. He's worth about $2,000 or more and knows it. He was given to me by Kathleen Atwater many years ago when most people hadn't heard about *Beanie Babies*. I think that she could be the inspiration for a character in a book, if her death hadn't been so tragic for all involved. I feel most sorry for her daughter. A vague memory surfaces of her serving me a chilled diet coke to go with my wine at a staff dinner in Kathleen's Durham home.

The bourbon arrives unexpectedly. I take a hearty swallow like a man expecting to find an oasis of inspiration for a Hemingwayesque story with short sentences packed with the power of a Mike Tyson punch, pounding the gut of our senses and sensibilities. Back off, Jane Austin.

That's when I remember; I don't drink. I choke on the warm liquid. My eyes water like a playground sissy, expecting the bully's smackdown at any moment. My fingers falter at the keyboard. The spellchecker yells at me for my string of nonsensical characters.

"What a wuss." Arnie chortles.

I realize now that I have to lay off the pistachios before bedtime.

~~~~~

The Shoelace

I found a fairly new white shoelace once. It lay there on the pebbled sidewalk in the noonday sun without its mate, curled into a pleasing smile. I thought about picking it up and taking it home, but what would I do with a single shoelace? It's like having one sock not matched to anything else. Still I wondered how it ended up here. It wasn't like someone bought it and it fell out of the grocery bag on the person's way home. It had been used ever so slightly.

Where it was creased, it retained its original brightness while the rest of it was off-white, eggshell, or some other color sold as a new brand of white. Who thinks of new brands of white? Perhaps it's someone with some Inuit blood in them who misses snow, and white appeals to them the way snow does, which has forty-two names in the Inuit language.

To me, white is white. The shoelace was white.

I sidestepped the shoelace to continue walking home. But a snap, sounding like a bull whip wielded by an angry Mexican lover jilted in the heat of passion, ricocheted in the air. The shoelace had tripped me with prejudice. I was tripped up, though I was really upside down.

I thought that was odd. Usually I end up on the ground when tripped by one of my own shoelaces, but there I was, suspended about six feet from the ground, my groceries deposited on the sidewalk, my eggs cracked, and an orange helplessly rolling downhill in the direction of a busy intersection.

I wondered about expressions we use in life, and

where they come from, tripped up, indeed. The shoelace lay on the ground below me; a frown replaced the smile.

"Fine. You made your point," I said.

I rotated like a Cirque du Soleil acrobat in mid-air and landed on my feet. I picked up the shoelace and searched for its mate, but never found it. I grabbed my scattered groceries and headed home.

There, I kicked off my sneakers once inside the house and put the remains of my groceries on the counter. I headed for my bedroom, and there, I placed the forlorn shoelace in my closet with all my other shoes and their attending laces. Seconds later, the floor of the closet was a tangled mess with the white shoelace in the center of it. The shoelace had found a home.

I guess even shoelaces don't like being abandoned, left behind, or lost. I walked back to the kitchen and surveyed my groceries. I thought about the orange rolling away all by itself. I laced up my sneakers and went back for it.

~~~~~

Documentaries

Rick coughed. He hit the mute button on the remote control. Coughed again.

Then, he really started to hack and the rocking chair he was sitting in moved back and forth and side to side on the hardwood floor like a spastic ride on the Midway all the while ignoring the sharp needle-pricking pain in his shoulder. When the coughing finally subsided, he hocked a loogie into a wad of tissue the size of a camel's hump.

Sydney, perched on Rick's shoulder, relaxed his claws and bit Rick's ear.

"Damn, that hurts," Rick said, knowing that the aged cockatiel was just reminding him that he didn't wish to partake in any more amusement rides.

Sydney fluffed his feathers. "Whatchadoing?"

"Hocking a green and red loogie." Rick showed Sydney the flu-generated mess.

Sydney didn't look.

"Don't worry. I won't give you People Flu."

Rick grabbed the remote control from the settee where it had been tossed during the wild coughing fit. Settling back into his seat, he placed it on the end table then poured another teaspoonful, in a long line of teaspoonfuls, of *Zutripro Solution*. He grimaced as he swallowed the foul tasting liquid. Sydney crawled down his arm and then hopped onto the end table. He nibbled the box of *Tamiflu*.

"Yeah, yeah. I know." Rick took the box away from Sydney, who hissed his displeasure. Rick popped one of the pills with a chaser of orange juice.

Sydney jumped on Rick's knee and started

41

grooming himself. Rick stared at the bottle of *Tylenol,* unsure when he'd taken the last pill. Five long days with almost no sleep from the unrelenting deathbed rattle of a cough had started to take its toll on Rick's memory. A programming change flickered on the silent television. Rick looked at Sydney.

"Now I remember. Take a *Tylenol* when the documentary starts. All hail, documentaries," Rick said with mock obedience to the television Gods. Sydney crawled back up Rick's body to his preferred shoulder position as Rick struggled with the childproof cap in order to extract a pill to take the edge off the aches in his bones.

Mission complete. Rick grabbed the remote.

"Whatchadoing?"

"Watching what promises to be one of the best documentaries of the day." He depressed the mute button.

"This is David Attenborough. Come join me in the southern United States, Arkansas specifically, where we will be hunting for an elusive monster that roams this still fairly remote part of America. And now, noodling for giant catfish."

"Told you it was going to be a good one." He coughed again. "I do so love documentaries." Rick sighed.

Sydney covered his face with a wing to hide his embarrassment.

~~~~~

A Brighter Day

I pull tight my oversized black hoodie to ward off the fat raindrops beating down on me. My navy blue sweat pants cling like the skin of the fat man after a great weight loss. Damn you, Maury Povich, for showing the world that image. It never leaves me. I shudder and continue my peg leg walk, leaning on my staff, to the hospital rehabilitation center to visit Pat. What little eye makeup I applied this morning runs its last. My physical therapy class had taken most of it. It was pure vanity on my part. The therapist is hunky, but not worth the raccoon eyes. A half-dozen more nubile bodies squirm under his steady guidance every day. Yet still, we all hang on to things precious until we're ready to let go.

The automated door swings open, and I limp past the receptionist's desk. She looks up. I don't acknowledge her. She's seen me pass by before, but I catch a look of disdain, no, revulsion. Screw her. I'm on a mission of mercy. It's not up to her to judge.

I enter the darkened room from the bright corridor and stand transfixed. Pat looks dead, yet her monitor beeps. Her oxygen generator hums loud enough to drown out most noise. How can someone sleep with that racket? But, she sleeps, or rather exists in an empty wakefulness most days, knowing she'll never recover from her various ailments. Still, the noise must be better than listening to her own death rattle, and yet, some days she begs me for a cigarette.

She is not her any longer – not inquisitive and opinionated, quoting Tolstoy or Angelou. What keeps this woman alive? Why do I visit weekly in my own pain this crotchety person who has virtually no one, because she learned not to bend from an unbendable parent eighty years ago?

Her eyes flutter open. She raises a bony finger in my direction. "Death," she gasps, but I might have only thought I heard her say it.

Eyes close. The arm drops. The monitor clangs. Footsteps rush. I retreat out of the room, and then walk away. Her son will begrudgingly drive from wherever to claim his estranged mother, now that she is dead.

Outside, the sun bursts through. Dull grey clouds reveal a deep blue Carolina sky. Revitalized trees shimmer as they shed water. A robin pounces on a late breakfast worm. The pain in my leg eases as I walk, as though a hand was massaging it from within. Pat's gone. My mood brightens, and I share her relief.

~~~~~

Shrink Wrapped

Ichbart stuck to the ceiling. His hundreds of tiny talons gripped the paneled ceiling like the Mexican cactus that he once fell in love with at first glance before she repelled him.

"Stupid weed," he mumbled, forgetting where he was at the moment and captured by a memory.

"Are we ready to talk," Dr. Manfreid Mann sat in a dark corner; his pen light blinded Ichbart.

"Point that thing elsewhere."

"Duly noted." The light dimmed and only the dull soft glow from the writing tablet lit the room.

Ichbart relaxed. "Two nights ago, I dreamt I was a wigwam, though I had to access the computer to understand what it was."

"I see."

Stupid human. He sees nothing. "Last night, I dreamt I was a teepee. In my readings about the wigwam, I remembered what that was. It was most unsettling. Houses made of animal skins or stretched bark. How barbaric."

"I see."

"Oh, please enlighten me." Ichbart could hardly contain his sarcasm. His faith in human psychiatric methodology had failed so far in providing a clue to his troubles.

"Well, on the surface, being so far from your home world, you're tense, too tense."

Ichbart heard the muffled smirk, but it took him a few seconds for the implications to register, before the left brain idiosyncratic processes communicated to the right brain's reactionary logic. "So, you're

45

cracking a joke at my expense, that I'm two tents."

"Well, yes. Just to loosen things up. To break the tension if you get my meaning."

Ichbart gathered himself together. Folding his extremities to approximate human form was always difficult on most days, but now it was proving impossible, as anger at being the butt of a joke overlaid his tenseness and anxiety. But finally, as he dropped from the ceiling and shed his thinly veiled human form, releasing himself from the confines, he understood the basic needs aspect of his issues. He understood the emptiness that plagued him, that gnawing hunger inside.

"Nice transformation." Dr. Mann glanced at his watch. "Are we ready to get serious? Other aliens are waiting for their counseling sessions."

"I'm ready," Ichbart said.

Dr. Mann was a big man. It will take a long time to digest this impotent ham.

~~~~~

Writing in the Big Arena

"Good evening, nouns and verbs. It's time for the WWW smackdown, Woeful Writers Writing. In this evening's match, up-and-coming writer, Rick Bylina, takes on evil incarnate, The Internal Editor. TIE has done just that with Bylina's creative juices, tying them up by making him think he's progressing by having him flip back and forth between -ed and -ing ending verbs while the clock ticks away.

Bylina has had some brilliant story moves that have shut down The Internal Editor's best efforts, but he seems to lack the stamina to make those moves last for 2,000 words a day for a month."

"He's a wimp," Muse Sharon Stone said.

"What makes you say that, Muse?

"Let me tell you, in the day, I'd have him rip off 2,000 words in two hours and then have him go to the mall in search of nubile babes that he couldn't have even if he were dressed in $100 dollar bills, all to build up the frustration for another round of writing. Nothing gets a writer moving better than sexual frustration."

"But The Internal Editor is one tough customer."

"TIE is a wuss. Look here, Adam Adverb. No TIE can stop a writer. Only a writer stops a writer. A TIE, no matter how forceful, is only as good as the words that are on the page. Take away the words, TIE crawls back to his backspace key like a dull eraser on an old pencil.

"So, your money is on the wimp?"

"Yeah, he's a wimp, but he's beaten TIE before,

he just needs some diet cokes and Little Debbie's cakes. Next week's match though ought to be a great one."

"You mean--"

"Yeap. WB returns."

"Holy cow plops. Well, we'll see how this one turns out, but next week; join us when WB, Writer's Block, returns to the ring to tussle with Bylina. WB has smacked down Bylina before, but I don't think Bylina fears him as much any longer. Same place, same time. This is Adam Adverb alongside Muse Sharon Stone, saying so long from Bylina's subconscious."

"You know, Adam, it can get really dark in here."

"Just head for the light; just head for the light."

~~~~~

A Boarish Affair

The parlor maid served Reginald another snifter of brandy, hoping it was the correct brand out of the hundreds he kept for just the right moment. He sipped and then furrowed his brow. "This is an evening brandy." He upturned the drink onto her tray. "Fetch me something for mid-morning."

She ran to the small liquor closet near the doors. Moments later, Reginald nodded, as if to take a nap. His head snapped up when his wife commented about the dinner menu not being set yet. He yawned. "This country air must be making me tired."

"You beast," Melody ejaculated, bolting upright from the settee. "You damn well know that you're implying I'm a bore. You've dismissed everything I've suggested we do these past few weeks for your brandy, port, and billiards with the boys."

"Now dearest," Reginald said, unsuccessfully stifling another yawn.

Melody rushed out the door to the gardens of her father's country estate, now being allowed to go to seed since Reginald had taken charge of the financial affairs after her father's death.

A wild boar bolted out of the thick hedge and knocked Melody over. A piece of cloth covering the boar's eyes, it charged into the parlor room. The maid saw the boar coming, screamed, and ran to the far corner of the room. Reginald threw down his paper. "What in the bloody blue blazes is going on? Kill the bloody thing, you incompetent twit. Then leave. You're fired. You should have shut the door when my wife went outside for some air." The boar turned and then charged Reginald, goring him in the stomach with his massive tusk.

The maid swung a fireplace poker and struck the bore. He was dead.

Melody charged into the room with a pitchfork like an Amazon warrior and dispatched the boar. She looked at Reginald. A solemn grin grew on her lips. She turned to the maid, cowering in the corner.

Tis Botany Bay for me now, she thought.

"Well done, maid. Ring the butcher and have him prepare the other white meat for supper. I'll get rid of the bore."

~~~~~

Mr. Jingles' Lecture

I used to belong to a book club. Several years ago, we read *The Green Mile* and were meeting that evening to discuss it.

However, that afternoon, about two hours before the meeting, I found a mouse in our large soaking tub. He could not get out. I live in the country and capture four or five mice in the attic after the first significant cold waves every year. I've only had two mice in the house, easily caught the next night with peanut butter and the ultimate mouse trap. But this guy, nope. He seemed special.

I picked him up and put him in a huge glass jar. Yes, I put holes in the lid, put in some bird seed, and a soaking wet piece of toilet paper for moisture. He seemed rather content on the drive over to the book club meeting.

He was our guest lecturer at the meeting, receiving, "Oh, so cute," comments from most of the attendees. But the host gave him a look of hatred. "They're nothing but pests, good only for cat food." She had farmed in her youth and had no patience for vermin.

Well, Mr. Jingles (what other name would you expect since we were discussing *The Green Mile*) sat in his glass prison for the evening, eating bits of oatmeal and raisin cookies deposited in the jar for him. At the end of the evening, we all trundled outside, and I gently coaxed Mr. Jingles out of the jar.

He went about two feet, and then turned around. He sat up on his back two feet, and I swear to God, he waved goodbye. He then scampered off into the nearby bushes.

Since then, we've never had another mouse in the house or the attic. Life goes that way sometimes.

The hostess, well, she was overwhelmed with mice during the winter, and actually had to move out for several weeks while the exterminators cleared them out.

"Musta taken years to make all these tunnels," one man said.

I wonder where Mr. Jingles is tonight.

(This, unlike the other stories in this book, is a true story.)

~~~~~

M&Ms on the Grass

(Or, how to start a literary novel that will be talked about for years.)

Unexpected heat arrived. Mind-numbing days slipped by, and I reached the boiling point. Killed. Puked. Got better. Did it again. Couldn't stop. They all teased. Women. Blood red lips gently whispering for me to take them away from their lives of quiet desperation making Betty Crocker pies and vacuuming for men who didn't appreciate their abs of steel, tight asses, and ample hooters. I appreciated them, many, many times to their silent delight.

Switched and dispatched men with excess testosterone, no taste, and bad breath. Retched without fail. Retched over success. Did more. Daily. Teenage mall cop popping zits nearly caught me. I stopped to poop with a victim's bloody head in a green plastic bag as though it were a ripe cabbage destined for Egg Foo Yong. It commingled in my Target reusable tote with my two-pound bag of M&Ms on sale for $1.99. Bargain. Melt in your mouth, not in your hands.

The heat that struck like a sirocco torching Tunis in the afternoon gave way to a dry, cold front that swept that nauseous air out to sea. I felt relief. I walked towards home with the tote bag after the sun went down, and the feeling was euphoric.

A full moon bathed the park--too cool for bugs; too warm for a coat--casting eclipse gray shadows of protective branches over a couple kanoodling: him begging, she capitulating, me watching. What's one more?

My knife blade glistened, but tree roots knotted my laces. I fell. Shock silenced my sudden pain; I uttered not a sound. Head rolled downhill. M&Ms scattered across the fescue. What a waste. All my heat dissipated into the cool Earth, knowing I didn't save her. She'd have morning sickness.

~~~~~

True Love

Queen Bea watched the king's blood flow and stain the floor. Then, she smiled and gave the blue knife back to Wren who wiped the blade clean. "It can do no more harm," the queen said to her fair maid. "He can't too." The queen squeezed Wren's arm. "Leave with my words and throw the knife in the moat."

Wren sensed the strength of the queen's words and had to think fast. "Yes, my queen."

She edged out the false door then fled to the Grand Hall. "Guards," Wren called out. "Men in black slew the king."

A knight's shout rang out. "Close the gates. Hunt these fools down." His voice turned cold. "God save the queen."

As the guards dashed from the hall, a sly grin grew on Wren's face. "They chase ghosts. I'll waste no tears for this weak, faint, and false king." She left to make plans.

Forced on the throne as a child bride to mend two foes, Queen Bea was a young teen when her son was born. That son was now a strong, brave, and true man, who now mourned his loss. The next night Queen Bea told Wren, "My son shall be a great king. And though some may think they know last night's truth, they do not. No one stops this plan."

"All will soon be as it should."

"I have no doubt," said the queen.

While March's cold warmed to May, the queen wept few tears for the dead king, and then wed the love of her loins. Late that night, the blue knife sank in the moat drenched with the queen's blood.

Long June days came. As planned, the new king wed his true love who wore white trimmed with blue and showed a sly grin.

(Author's note: Contest winner for a 300-word maximum short story using only single-syllable words. Did you notice that fact?)

~~~~~

End of Days

The end of days came and went. At the last toll of twelve, the high priest slammed his hand on the rock slab. "Just wait!" His large flock cried through the night and the first hours of the next day. They stayed out of fear or love for their faith.

"The gods can't be wrong," the Priest said to his flock. "Stay and pray." With that, he walked to his tent.

Some of the flock left. Most stayed to hear what the priest would say when he came back; and when he did, those who left ran back scared. The flock grew and filled the field.

The priest stood on a knob at high sun. "Good news. The date is six months hence. Go. Be of good cheer."

A tall man stood at the field's edge. "I gave up my wife, child, and crops to come. I must wait six more months?"

The priest squirmed in place. "For some, six months can seem like a breath. All! Bless this man for what he has done for the gods."

The flock was quiet.

"Bless this man, I say."

Just then, the moon slid in front of the sun and the light dimmed. The flock bowed low and moaned in awe.

The moon let the sun live, but on the knob, the priest lay with a spear through him.

An old man kicked the priest. "No breath. He's dead."

The flock saw that the tall man stood proud, sans

his spear.

The old man yelled, "Bless this man. He made end of days true for the priest. Let the count of days start once more." The old man carved the date of the new end of days in the priest's rock slab: one two two one one two.

(Author's note: Another 300-word maximum short story using only single-syllable words. Did you notice that fact?)

~~~~~

Holiday Spirit

I'm so not in the holiday spirit. It's ninety-four degrees at noon. The AC is yelling, "Not again." The birdbath, filled at 6 a.m., is now nearly depleted from all the birds drinking or splashing around in the life-giving water. The parched earth cracks under my car, threatening to devour it like a carnivore with a relentless appetite.

I should move the car, but I can't touch the handle due to the excessive heat. The burns from last year are just about healed. The vinyl seats are melting faster than the Wicked Witch of the West. Soon, the material will flow lava-like beneath the doors.

Flowers lean uncharacteristically toward the shade. In the morning, I hear their plaintive whispers of, "Water. Please, water."

Only the okra rises above the dead and the dying, thrusting its purple flowers skyward while its roots wring the last molecules of water from the dirt clods beneath it. Happy red-headed turkey vultures eat the dead creatures in my backyard, piled up like the end of a lemming march to the sea; the ones that couldn't make their goal; the ones providing a succulent last meal to the higher orders of the food chain before mass starvation sets in.

In this shimmering landscape, with its mirrored echoes of water shimmering in the distance, you ask us to write something uplifting and in the holiday mood?

Well, I could imagine I'm in Alice Springs, Australia for the Christmas holidays.

"G'day mate, hope Santie arrives all-in on the

back of that croc with a kangaroo pouch full of tucker."

Imagination is my only weapon now. The world is on fire, paper burns away, and my pen has just melted.

~~~~~

Romance by the Sea

"John," she murmured breathlessly. Don't go, she thought, grasping his hand harder than the town idiot when he cracks walnuts.

"Mary. God, I don't want to leave, but I must," he said through gritted teeth as she crushed his fingers with her grip. My past is catching up to me, he lamented internally.

"Stay." Should I tell him I know of his past? No. He's too proud. He'd hate my snooping. I never noticed how soft his fingers were, like a cow's teat.

"I'm going." If only she'd find out on her own about my past and my misgivings.

The launch bobbed up and down. Mary had to let her tenuous grip on John ooze away like melted butter on a summer's day. His crushed fingers twittered a feeble goodbye.

I should beg him once more, but I won't torture him.

If only she'd ask me again, I'd stay, but she's too proud.

The strong tide pulled the launch to the clipper ship bound for Australia. Eight thousand miles would separate us, John thought. "What's that noise, Quartermaster Quint?"

"DUM DUM. DUM DUM. DUM DUM DUM DUM DUM DUM."

Quint winked at John. "Tis just the sea."

"No," John responded. "Tis the pounding of Mary's broken heart."

Mary slipped to the ground her heart beating wildly, as she watched the small launch grow smaller, dip in the swells, rise over the waves. She had to look away. She was getting quesy.

"I just know evil lurks out there." She picked up a sea cucumber and bit into it to quell the gnawing of the bitter separation between them like a hunger that can't be satisfied. She spit it out.

"As God is my witness, I shall never eat that again."

~~~~~

Shopping for Love

Maria and I were through. This also meant I went back to shopping again, but that was okay. The sex had been hot, often, and good, but I didn't share her love for aisle 9: Tex-Mex, hot stuff, weird textured foods, and her friends talking up the mouth-burning foods as though they enjoyed seared tonsils.

Aisle 8 we split. She hoarded cans of whatever; I enjoyed cereal in the morning: *Grape Nuts*, *Cheerios*, and the occasional wrestling match with Tony the Tiger. "*Frosted Flakes*, they're great." I look around to see if anyone heard my mumbled shout of delight. Coast was clear.

Aisle 10 was like a lost friend I hadn't seen in the past seven months of our whirlwind, turbulent romp. Vegetables and fruits, the deli, and the bread bar. I was home in aisle 10 and exuberantly filled the cart with my favorites. I picked up a pair of melons. While judging them, I pushed my cart a bit too hard with my hips in the direction of check-out.

Clank!

She stood there, staring at my cart, t-boned into hers.

"I'm sorry." I hooked the bottom of my cart with my foot, pulling it back.

"Nice pair." She pointed to my melons. A dimpled smile formed. I swear her blue eyes twinkled.

She held a ripe banana by the stem. I couldn't resist. "Is that a banana or are you happy to see me?"

She blushed. "I'm Mary." She pointed her banana at my cart. "It's nice to meet a guy who eats something other than Tex-Mex."

63

~~~~~

Love and the Single Girl

Dr. Frankenberry stared at the jellyfish and wondered if they were staring back.

"They're beautiful," he said to Inga.

"Oh, let me go. You're mad." Inga, clad in a leopard skin bikini, which the doctor bought from Macy's using a seasonal coupon, jingled her silvery chains. "Pretty," she said, before remembering her situation.

"Just think," the doctor said, filling a needle with fluid from a jellyfish that writhed in obvious pain, "if this works, you'll be young and beautiful forever."

"I want to be free," she said emphatically.

The doctor added a yellow fluid into the needle, and then injected her. He waited. He waited for hours. Nothing happened. Inga finally went to sleep and snored like the town drunk on Sunday morning.

"Drat!" He turned to his desk then sat. He immersed himself in his notes, looking for what could have gone wrong. Hours passed.

He pushed his glasses up to the bridge of his nose. A squishy sound erupted from behind him.

He turned.

"My God!"

Inga slipped out of her silvery bracelets and approached the doctor, stinging him repeatedly before consuming him. She turned to the wounded jellyfish in the tank, slipped inside the aquarium, and made sweet love to her wounded hero.

~~~~~

65

The Ant Eater

Ben sat on the warm sidewalk, the sun to his back, and a bottle in his hand. He tipped it up on occasion, when thirst nipped at his throat. Early summer: warmth without oppressive humidity, breezes without the blow dryer affect, and a rebirth of life. With so many competing fragrances in the air, it was hard for him to focus on one. All this was true, but Ben's focus settled on a line of ants following some trail known only to them. Ben surely didn't know about it.

Then, the monster approached. Ben's eyes opened wide. The monster gobbled up the ants one by one as they passed in front of its wide mouth. It was as though the ants were on a conveyor belt at a buffet line passing by a single, hungry customer.

Thoroughly upset, Ben lifted his hand and slammed it down on the monster. "Bad bug!" he yelled, and repeatedly pounded the bad bug into oblivion.

"No, Ben," his startled mama said. "Toad."

She picked up her two-year-old, and then took him inside to wash the remains of the squashed amphibian off his hand.

~~~~~

All's Right with the World

"Wait!" The dog barked.

"What's up, Lassie? What is it?" Timmy asked.

Stupid human, Lassie thought.

Stupid mutt. Timmy exhaled.

"There's a rattlesnake behind that tree, you Moron," Lassie barked enthusiastically.

"Want to play fetch. Here, chase this stick. Stick!" Timmy threw the stick.

Lassie dashed after the irresistible piece of oak that a dozen squirrels, two possums, and one raccoon had used to mark their territories. She found the olfactorily delightful stick, and then turned around just in time to see Timmy lie down on the snake.

Timmy screamed. Lassie barked. The stick fell to the forest floor. The snake slithered away. Lassie ran back to Timmy, bit him on the arm, and sucked out the poison as best he could.

A squirrel in a tree chattered, "Dog!" All the squirrels froze in place.

Timmy died from the snake bite. Dogs can't really suck anything. Lassie was set to be put down, deemed a vicious dog, but escaped to live free with the wolves of Fundy Bay. The squirrel became owl food. The snake ate the baby owlets. A smiling God watched on high from his orthopedic mattress set at 43 for firm comfort.

~~~~~

Sex

Rick stared at the paper, burning his fingertips with promise.

Despite his concentration, he could still hear his gang outside in the yard milling about, talking nonsense as they waited for him. The paper cooled, and he mused that his motley crew, Arnie, Cindy, Ben, Amy, Carol, and Etcsy, would wait for a long time for him. At fifteen, though, he felt a compulsion to deal with the bad girl that had left him the pages.

The promise of her, the newness, the possibilities enticed him like none had before. Even Annie, with whom he had shared some quiet moments with kisses verging on the French style he'd read about, didn't seem to pull on his yearnings as much as the words before him and the adventure in a lusty discovery that beckoned.

He slipped out the side door and bolted for the woods, glancing back once to make sure no one followed. They didn't see him go. He disappeared through the small meadow and entered the lushness of her promise.

~~~~~

A True Hero

My writing computer is old. His name is
Raymond. I've been neglectful about backing up
Raymond. This morning, after ten years of faithful
service, Raymond had a massive heart attack along
with a stroke that was exacerbated by a total
shutdown of the liver and kidneys. In short, Raymond
died a horrible death.

The service doctor has pronounced him dead.
"Bury him in China after retrieving the gold and silver
within."

Raymond was a noble computer, a brave
computer, a computer who never complained.
Raymond had my back and needs a more fitting send-
off. Raymond needs the computer version of the
Medal of Honor, the Freedom Medal, and the Legion
of France. Why? Raymond allowed me to finish my
back up five minutes before dying, saving five novels,
forty-two short stories, and so much more in the
process.

Long live Raymond in the computer version of
the afterlife.

Excuse me. I must go grieve.

~~~~~

A Real Emergency

"Nine-one-one. State the nature of your emergency."

"Well, my brother-in-law is coming in a few weeks."

"Sir, that is not an emergency."

"Well, you haven't met him."

"Are you in danger?"

"No, but my plumbing system surely is. Oh, yeah, and my six-month supply of food might not make it six days. Oh, my God!"

"Is there a problem, sir?"

"My home theater. He just looks at it and my reds become orange and my blues violet."

"Sir, that sounds like a personal problem not a reason to call nine-one-one."

"But you don't understand."

"What don't I understand, sir?"

"He's a salesman. He might sell me something I don't want that he doesn't understand and I don't need and can't pay for."

"Dispatching the SWAT team, immediately. Stay inside. Lock the doors. And stay on the line until they arrive."

"Thank you."

"You're welcome. Just don't give him my name."

~~~~~

Sometimes Even Writers Get the Blues

He typed the last words while the beast pounded at his door. It wouldn't be long before the door would crack open like a fresh egg. He only hoped that the secret message inside the email would find its way to the recipient. He couldn't risk stating it in clear text. The fate of the publishing world, and in fact, the entire world rested on the receiver understanding the choices to be made.

The door split open. The writer faced his tormentor.

With sharpened quill dripping ink in one hand and a thesaurus with worn pages in the other, the demon muse stood there with a sardonic smile etched on his pustulated face. "Are you ready?"

The writer sighed. "Why can't my muse look like Sharon Stone?"

~~~~~

71

Winter Lovers Torn Asunder

February 2, 1887, Fred and Ernie lay in blissful slumber in the frosty domain until the mayor of Punxsutawney ripped Fred from his beloved partner, held him up in front of a bunch of drunken Methodists, and proclaimed, "Six more weeks of Winter. Let's eat."

Ernie bit the mayor on the ankle. Fred wiggled free. They dove for cover, deeper than ever before in their hidey-hole where they lay in a loving embrace for another six weeks.

The mayor told a different story.

~~~~~

Simple Misunderstandings

"Are the knives sharp?" Frank put on his coat.
"They could split an Adam."
Frank looked over at Johnny. "Atom."
"Yeah, Adam."
"Whatever." Frank opened the door, and they departed.

After they dispatched Adam, Frank tossed the knives down the old well just as a Higgs boson God particle escaped from the CERN facility and passed by. The explosion could be felt five hundred miles away.

~~~~~

Love on the Cuff

"Bill!" Mary locked lips with him, ripped off his clothes, and made passionate love with him for three minutes in the dark, back hallway of her luxury apartment house.

Prying his lips from hers, he shouted breathlessly, "But, I'm not Bill."

"You bastard, taking advantage of me like that."

"But it was fantastic!" he ejaculated.

"Yes, it was," she gushed.

"Marry me?"

"Okay."

~~~~~

A Word Writers Never Use Anymore

It was a bright and peaceful day. I was happy about our trip together. The ship glided over the calm ocean waters with the grace of a swan in a reflecting pool.

Then, the first mate ejaculated, "Dead man, swimming."

And so he wasn't!

I wasn't gay anymore.

~~~~~

All is Not Right with God

God gave, left, returned. Cried inconsolably.

~~~~~

Forrest Gimp

Helen felt the ground under her rumble, vibrating her bare feet. "Run, Forrest. Run," she mumbled unintelligibly.

Despite Ms. Keller's encouragement, the train rolled by faster than a bullet. Poor Forrest, she lamented.

Ms. Sullivan arrived the next day.

(First draft of "Forrest Gump" found while dumpster diving. Proof that even great stories have to start somewhere.)

~~~~~

Writer's Insight

My pen kissed the blank sheet of paper, and I exclaimed, "The greatest novel ever written is just being started."

Before she left the room, my wife snickered, "Great. When you find out who's writing it, let me know."

She died fast, without seeing it coming.

I died slow, after years of rejections.

~~~~~

Owe That Dog a Bone

even before i pull down the black bag Fluffy knows i am going he would shred it but he fears it

the black suitcase masters me

a neighborly wave i am gone wishin i had time for one more cup of joe one more cinnamon roll one more warm embrace one more walk around the place but the cold air smacks me awake and the crossroads of america beckon

i waved at someone on another bus opposite heading

could we switch rides for the joys of coming home

i unpack black bag and a hard rubber chew bone drops out guess he figured an offering to the black bag might keep me home

i owe that dog a bone

~~~~~

Television Viewing at Night

Twilight played on the DVD all night long, over and over again due to some bug in the software. Sydney, my twenty-year-old cockatiel, watched. He couldn't help it. The television stood just a few feet away from where he'd landed the evening before, and he didn't like flying during the night though he loved the way these humans, bats, and werewolves seemed untethered to Newton's theory of gravity as he understood it.

At six in the morning, the power flickered off. The television went silent. The graying of the morning began.

Sydney felt the urge. He flew. He dove. He swooped. He landed on Rick's neck and bit hard, drinking in the blood while thinking, who needs two fangs when one beak will do.

~~~~~

80

The Day Timmy Found a Polar Bear

Rain lashed the area, but when Timmy saw the polar bear wash into his backyard on top of a Vega, he just had to disobey his stepmom and investigate. He waited for her to leave for the store to buy a loaf of bread.

By then, the bear had left the Vega. When Timmy spotted him again, the bear seemed tired, lying on the shed just like Snoopy, paws dangling down, tail dripping water, and eyes closed. Timmy wandered up to the white bear with paws stained brown from the mud and red from cuts from sharp objects Timmy could only imagine.

"Poor bear," Timmy said, petting a paw larger than his head.

The bear gurgled a grunt. A swollen eyelid lifted.

Timmy looked at the bear. "Are you hungry?"

The bear looked at the writer. "Do you really want to go on with this?"

~~~~~

Fateful Decisions

With unabashed sadness, the monsoon of tears erupted from her hazel eyes, flowing down her face unabated, streaking indifferently her dark mascara, and lingering with regret on her chin before dropping to stain her red blouse. She shuddered and drew her burgundy jacket close to hide from prying eyes that knew the truth, suspected the truth, or suspended judgment absorbed in their empathetic grief. Gusty winds blew away comforting words like the last dead leaves that flittered across the grounds from a nearby shivering oak.

He stood so close, his aftershave wafted over her in waves, but yet a sliver of morning light sliced between them and shined on the small graveside plaque. She wrapped her fingers tightly around his hand seeking a touch of warmth and found none, realizing now that she knew for sure. The decision to terminate had not been mutual after all.

~~~~~

Zombie Erotica

You stare blankly, uncaring, as her top tumbles down. Your unkempt fingernails rake her blonde mane. She is afraid. Good. No. Bad. No. Dang! You can't remember anything except that you have an urge you haven't felt since you were raised from the world of worms and grubs.

You corner her on the bed. Rip! No more bikini bottom. She doesn't yell. Too scared? Maybe she enjoys this. Good. Piercing noises hurt. Moans echo in the bare room. Hers? Yours? The cat you've just crushed. She turns her head away; eyes closed. There is no resistance.

Your tongue licks her lips. Damn! You wish you still had the rest of your tongue, not to mention your lips. What's that smell? The last of your olfactory senses kick in. The crushed cat? No. Brains. No. No. Don't do this to me, I'm almost there.

Brains or sex. Brains or sex. What the heck? Sex, then brains.

Now what's fallen off?

Drat to Hades! Okay, only brains.

~~~~~

A Powerful Will

My house was a jail, a prison, a tomb. I was sealed inside tight with the shades drawn, doors and windows locked, and all household appliances switched off. Even the wood stove had no fire. I was safe.

I knew I shouldn't, but I pulled back the corner of the window shade to look outside anyway, just to verify they were there. It was a fatal error! They detected me.

They started to come. I couldn't turn away as I continued to look out my portal to the outside. I watched the endless hordes march relentlessly toward my house, their faces concealed in the shadows. Light from the streetlight at dusk behind them, sketched their shadowy outline on the sidewalk, which grew longer, the closer they approached.

In moments, they were at my front door; seconds later, they were at the back door. Hundreds of tiny hands rapped at the doors and unmercifully pressed the doorbell until the noise was deafening. It overpowered my defenses.

I could no longer hide, I could no longer resist. I ran to the front door. My heart pounded and the veins on my forehead stood out as I opened it. Then, a hundred million voices screamed out in unison, "Want to buy some *Girl Scout* cookies?"

Resigned to my fate, I replied, "Give me three boxes of each."

~~~~~

Death Due to Roll-on

"Death, Dr. Watson, was caused by arsenic poisoning."

"Not very clever, Holmes."

"Actually, quite clever. The killer had everyone suspecting the son, daughter, friend, visitor, everyone but the one person who wasn't there."

"Come now, Holmes, Lady Ashtabulaworthshire has been in London for a month."

"Quite right, my dear Watson. More than enough time for Sir Randolph Ashtabulaworthshire the Tenth to go through a stick of deodorant laced with arsenic, thus applying his own murder weapon."

"That really stinks," Inspector Tutototemscone said, slapping the cuffs on Lady Ashtabulaworthshire. "But how did you know?"

"Elementary. It was by the stains under his shirt and basic chemistry. Arsenic and aluminum cancel each other out as a drying agent, so he sweated liberally instead of being as dry as a cucumber as any overpaid and underworked barrister should be. His own stench drove him to use more and more deodorant, until he overdosed on it. With the deodorant used up, the evidence disappeared before our noses. Had the maid not been killed by that oversized hound in the Baskerville swamp, what a pity for her, she would have washed all the evidence away with the laundry, which is where you'll find the evidence you need Inspector."

"He was main-lining his deodorant by the end," Watson said, shaking his head while pulling at his mustache.

"Precisely," Holmes responded.

~~~~~

First Reaction is Usually Correct

I should kill it right now.

The tick crossed my arm looking for a tender spot. Maybe it could sense where the blood rose closest to the surface of my skin. Maybe my hairy arms made maneuvering the multiple legs difficult. Maybe it wasn't hungry and just looking for a resting spot. Maybe it was very hungry and disoriented, having been swept away from its perch upon some blade of grass, a deer's ass, or some other organic mass this morning while I worked in the garden.

Perhaps the tick was pregnant and looking for a place to birth her ticklets---a rather revolting thought. A public television special about the mother spider giving up its life by allowing her children to eat her came to mind. I wondered if ticks did the same thing.

As it reached the soft side of the elbow joint, that last image disgusted and horrified me. I couldn't let this tick latch on. I've already had Lyme disease twice, and the medication was an unpleasant intrusion into my life. Still, I watched the tick on its endless trek. Does it know I'm food? Does it know it's being hunted? Does it know Pythagorean's Theorem?

The timer chimed in the kitchen. My breakfast was almost ready.

I grabbed the tick with tweezers. Over the sink, I lit a match. It popped. And then, I washed it down the drain before I took my shower.

What else did anyone expect me to do with a tick? Name it?

~~~~~

87

Sydney

(My twenty-year-old cockatiel, Sydney, begged to have his story included. Here it is.)

Bright lights. Someone comes. It is early. Darkness outside. On my purse, gawd, I love my soft cloth purse, I stretch. Food. Now. Can't they hear me? I've been yelling politely for ten seconds. Ah, Cheerios. Ah, a cashew. Is it my birthday? Oh, the joy. Millet seed. Crunch, snap, pop, snarf. Wait a minute. Every time they give me millet. Wait. Ah, good bowel movement. Where was I? Millet. Delicious, wondrous. Wait a minute. Every time they give me. Ooh. A finger. Oh, I love being on shoulders. Ear lobe. Hey! If I want to nibble, I'll nibble. Damn hand, but the purse is soft. Ooh. Millet. Snarf, gobble, chew. Wait a minute. Every time they. Fresh water. I drink the sweet nectar and shout its goodness. Ooh. Millet. Ooh. A finger. I can't choose! Up and away on the shoulder again. Yes. To the office. Yes. Ah, that was a good poop. Tissue paper. Get away. Back down on office purse. Bare toes. Attack. Attack. Up and away. No, not the kitchen. No, I want the office. Not the kitchen purse. Ooh. Millet. Crack, fresh, 2011 is a good year. What's a year? I'm tired. My cardboard box. Darkness. Chewed cardboard is soft underneath. It was a hard morning. I yawn. Yawn. Yawn. Eyes heavy. Sneeze. Sneeze. Ah. Sleep, perhaps to dream. Yawn. I have to remember. Yawn. Remember sleep. Eyes close.

~~~~~

Aaron Anderson

Aaron Anderson returned.

After seven years, thirty-two days, and some odd hours, the dead man wandered through the back door of the house he had once owned and into the kitchen. He poured a cup of coffee. Aaron sat down on a chair he milled years ago at the small, round wooden table he'd created with his own hands in the shed outback.

Jenny, his daughter, didn't go into hysterics, faint, or approach him. Without looking away from his worn face covered with stubble, she picked up her cell phone and dialed 911.

"Aaron Anderson is in my kitchen. Please come."

She stayed on the line with the cops as instructed. His lean and long fingers embraced the steaming cup. Without a coat, she figured he must be cold, coming inside from the morning's nip.

Aaron Anderson carried the stench of death. His shirt was many sizes too large. His pants hung low, barely on. He parted his lips as if to speak to give life to his apparition. Seconds like minutes; minutes like hours, she waited. Her jumble of emotions couldn't settle. She beat back any pretense that she was glad to see him, but here he was. His steady gaze dropped from her to the cup. After a sip, his eyes shifted in the direction of an approaching siren.

He looked her in the eye once more then slid a key across the table to her, "I'm sorry." He folded his arms on the table and laid his head in them.

Aaron Anderson died once more.

~~~~~

Sex and the Single Zombie

"Ummm brains."

"God, you're the ugliest, slowest, deadest looking thing out on the street. But right now, you seem to be the only action in this sad sack section of the city. Looking for some action?"

"Ummm brains."

"Yes, honey. I hear you. And I want to be known for more than this smoking hot body I've labored to mold with Pilates, yoga, free-spinning, and hours with Franz and Hanz in the gym, tightening those sagging under arms."

"Ummm brains."

"Don't you go pawing the merchandise. I can lay you out."

"Ummm brains."

"Damn you need a bath, some mouthwash, and a shampoo. Don't you know the first rule? No tongues. And when was the last time you clipped those nails?"

"Brains?"

"That's it. Look at them. I haven't seen fingernails that long since the woman sprinter. Oh, what was her name?"

"Brains?"

"Flo Jo. That's it. Hey, back off, Jack."

"Ummm brains."

"Now, where are you going? That's it. Just walk away. Don't want your stinky, slow-witted butt anyway. I have standards."

"Ummm brains."

"That's it. Go get some of that slow-witted white meat over there."

"Ummm brains."

"Girl. Oh my God. Stop that screaming. Crap! Did you break a heel? That's right. Let old Mr. Brains help you up. I'm outta here. Gotta be something better around the next corner."

"Brains!"

"Why don't you two get a hotel room? Making all that fuss in an alley. Uh huh! I can still hear you? Comes another nice honey."

"BRAINS!"

"Damn. Look at that fine man." Stay calm. Oh, he's got the fever. I can tell he wants me already.

"BRAINS!"

"Hey sugar. Slow down. No! Oh, oh, oh. Stop that. Let go of my hair. Ow! I'm bleeding. You be crazy. You're ripping my head off, you jerk. Leave me…."

"No BRAINS."

~~~~~

I Told You So

Gail sat on the curb as the bus left the stop. It roared up the street to its next stop miles from here, and here was miles from where she hoped to be. No moon shined and a lone bulb blinked for the moths and said to the brown bats, "Food!"

She searched her purse. "Drink and cake," but her words fell to the ground in a heap. "Oh!" She drank and ate them at the last stop. She rubbed her bruised thighs.

A dull pop. She jumped up. The bus chugged past the edge of her known world, dipped, rose once more, and then its lights were gone. Now what?

She sought the end of the earth. That would teach them and save her. She glanced at the stars. This was close, but the high plains had no place for a teen to hide. The hills had huts, boys, trees, and snow. She liked snow; they did not.

Like a sketch of a corpse, a brick wall showed a house long gone. She checked it out, and then used a tin roof slat as a shield. She slept through the pain.

The tin came off with a whoosh. A bright light shined on her. She backed up, but a hand reached out to her and a calm voice said, "It's not what you think. You'll be fine." She stood with a brave face and saw dawn kiss the hills to the west. She had been so close to her goal.

When she had fled home, she said this was how it would end. The warm light grew in strength. She wept out of fear of what was to come, and then out of joy at the loss of pain. She rose in the light to the ship.

(Author's note: Another 300-word maximum short story using only single-syllable words. Did you notice that fact?)

~~~~~

True Passion

"Write!" Bubba was a man of few spoken words. He was also the best, fairest-priced mechanic in the tri-county area. He scribbled with his Number 2 pencil on a yellow legal pad smudged with grease from the brake job on which he'd been working.

An hour later, he put down the pencil, worn to the nub, next to the pile of paper. His large loopy handwriting covered the pages. He smiled in my direction with a great degree of satisfaction and nodded nearly imperceptibly that he was done. He then gently pulled a stick of gum from a pack like a debutante pulling a tissue from her sleeve. Bubba growled with satisfaction as he chewed it. He stood and stretched like a panther ready to pounce on an unsuspecting gazelle.

With six lengthy strides, Bubba stood before my car with his large hands, calloused in ways not normally associated with a mechanic. Bubba finished the brake job then hoisted the wheel back onto my Ford Explorer. He flipped on the compressor and grabbed the pneumatic wrench. Bubba tightened the lug nuts, and then lowered the car.

"Done," he said.

"Thanks." I looked him in the eye. "Sometimes you just have to strike...." I let the garage's exhaust fan suck the rest of the cliché away like a rank fart in a small bathroom.

"'Nuff said." He took my check.

As I drove away, I saw him get another pencil and pad. He plopped them beside his stool before he raised the next car. "Preparation is the key," he once said to me. Work from the long line of tired and patient customers would keep him busy until late at night.

A good mechanic is hard to find – a good writer, much rarer. I can't wait to read his next book.

~~~~~

I Don't Love PETA, But

I affixed my cigarette into the cigarette holder and lit it, glaring at him. Finally, I answered his insipid question: "The truth of the matter is, I didn't save Freddie's life. He was a bore. He couldn't write, dance, or sing, and yet, he still made it on *Dancing with the Stars* because of his tortured environmental past, saving earthworms from being used as fish bait."

A bat appeared out of the dark and guavo landed on my cigarette holder. It didn't stop me from continuing. "He became a billionaire with his alternative creation, a yeast-based fish bait spray, *Beauty Bait.*"

"Holy bat turds! But didn't---"

"But nothing, that lazy bum ruined my bait shack." I flicked the guano from the cigarette holder and the ashes off the tip of my cigarette. "I told the PETA people who were pushing Freddie's product that fish still felt the pain. His bait didn't numb them on contact. I had the proof, and Freddie knew I knew the truth.

"Oh, gawd!"

"Yep. And then I told them where to find Freddie."

"You mean?"

"The PETA people were hopping mad. They tried to suffocate him with alfalfa sprouts. They didn't succeed."

He gasped. "You mean?"

"Yes, damnit!" I threw down my cigarette. "I found him sprawled on the floor half choking, half laughing, realizing that the gig was up. He no longer belonged in our world or theirs. I sprayed the fish bait into his mouth to make it look like suicide to let the PETA people think they did something good for a change."

"That's incredible, but why are you confessing to me."

"I don't know--to set the record straight--to get the truth out." I hooked my thumbs on my vest pocket and eyed the cop. "No. It wasn't the PETA that killed him; it was *Beauty* that killed with yeast.

~~~~~

Practical Gifts

Despite his crippling arthritis, Reginald went to his knees in front of Naomi.

"Naomi. Marry me." Reginald felt his knees locking into position and knew he wouldn't be able to get up. He was stuck.

Naomi's mouth opened wider than a blue whale's with surprise. She clamped her eyes shut to hold back her tears of joy while sticking out her hand in obvious expectation of him slipping on the ring. She shook her long auburn locks, curled and gleaming from the essence of honey shampoo that always tickled his nose during close encounters of the loving kind. Then she smiled. Reginald could not hold his position when he raised his arm abruptly to deflect the brilliance of her teeth. He toppled over, landing with several dull thuds, like a heavy side of beef on the butcher's floor. He had knocked the wind out of himself.

"I can feel the pounding of my heart," she said. Her other hand slapped her ample breasts. "Yes! Today!" she shouted with her face turned to the Heavens in obvious delight. Her hand flickered back and forth in anticipation of him grabbing it.

"Oh," he gasped. "Oh." He attempted to speak through the pain of his knees and lack of air in his lungs.

"No?" Her response was quick and true for a woman scorned. "Well, I never have been so humiliated." She turned without looking and stomped out of his living room. He writhed in pain and knew when she jangled her keys that she was leaving, taking his house key with her.

Fire burned in Reginald's knees, as his legs remained locked in the L position. His breath came back in short, sharp gasps. He crawled to the window and opened it a crack. "Knees," he yelled.

Naomi's keys came crashing through the window. He stared at them, realizing that a hearing aid would have been a more practical Christmas gift for Naomi than teeth whitening treatments.

~~~~~

Reversal of Fortune

"Wait. Stop," Bob Witherspoon yelled.

The man, who had brushed by Bob moments ago, hesitated. One well-manicured hand clutched the silver door handle to a 2008 four-door, burgundy Grand Prix; the other, a fist full of off-white envelopes. The man's companion yelled, "Get in." His voice sounded rough, like someone who had not slept for days.

Bob ran the few steps to the man. "You dropped one of your envelopes."

The well-dressed man in a dark brown suit spun around to face Bob. He thumbed the bulging business envelopes. "Nine," he said. The coloring of his face turned from flushed red to ashen white. His blue eyes focused on the partially torn open envelope Bob held, revealing a wad of hundred dollar bills. The thick purple rubber band held them together.

Bob handed the man the money. "That's a lot of money to lose."

"For my honeymoon," the man blurted out.

"And I'm the best man who has to get him to the church on time," his partner said. "Get in." The man did as requested.

"Thanks," the man said, as the car peeled away, leaving a small trail of rubber behind. Dirt nearly hid the license plate of the otherwise pristine car.

"No problem." Bob waved at the men in the car, heading down the street. Alarms exploded from the bank behind Bob.

Bob sat in the police station interview room. Bank employees had pointed him out as the person

101

who helped the men get away. The police weren't gentle with him when they arrested him. It didn't help that Bob was shocked into silence by the turn of events. Stress had that effect on the mild-mannered man. But now, hours later, Detective Sergeant Arnold Schwimmer asked him a simple question.

"Can you tell us anything about the robbers?"

A sly grin grew on Bob's face. "I can tell you everything about them. I'm an expert in the field of memorization."

~~~~~

He's no Vegan

A twig snapped behind me as I stood at the edge of the vegetable garden. I whirled around.

"Crikey, a T-Rex," I mumbled too afraid to run or scream.

The giant emerged from the woods, sniffing the air. I remembered reading that the ugly brown and red drooling beast with twiggy arms and smelly breath flowing out of his slobbering mouth had poor vision. I stood still as a naked mannequin in a downtown department store window. I tried to remain frozen stiff---imaging the story grandfather told me about a day so cold that they had to have someone watch the fire to make sure it didn't freeze.

The T-Rex roared like Jackie Gleason after eating a Thai pepper. His yellow eyes stared at me as though I was a tuna surprise, yet I did not move a nostril hair. He sniffed me like a florist in a rose garden. The yellowed, foot-long teeth created the urge in me to floss them with rope. I resisted. In a blink, the twenty-five-foot tall beast leaned over into the garden and pulled up a row of my Early Surprise corn. He chewed it up. He sucked up twelve stalks of okra. The sound of satisfaction dribbled out of his mouth like Dom DeLuise at a breakfast buffet table.

I sighed in relief while watching him eat the garden though I knew my wife would be upset that her prized Napa Cabbage was now gone, along with the beanstalks. His pupils dilated as he eyed me. My shoulders dipped, and he caught the movement.

"Are you going to eat those carrots," he asked, with a voice that sounded a bit like Sean Connery's.

I shook my head and moved aside just as he scooped up fifty or so carrots near where I was standing. Relief overcame me. "You're a vegetarian?"

"Well, my cholesterol is a bit high." He slurped down the last of the carrots. "However, I mix things up most days." He smacked his lips and bent over.

~~~~~

Stuck in the Middle of the Middle of Everything

Statistically, age ten is the safest, but I can't vouch for it. At ten, I won a three-legged race at the Neshanic Station Volunteer Firemen's Picnic, but there was only one trophy. Planning for the prizes had eluded the firemen.

"Let your sister have it," Mom said. "She's younger."

Later, I was nearly run over by an angry cow and fell in a mud pit that was only partly mud.

"Stop annoying that cow," Dad said. "He's bigger than you."

Because of my fall, we left earlier than expected. On the ride home, my father drove in silence, puffing on his Lucky Strikes, one short-sleeved arm hanging out the window like the cool guy he was. My mom talked in short angry bursts about adult stuff, but her words flew out her window.

My older brother punched me every five minutes in my right arm for ruining the day. I think he was mad because he and my Aunt Joannie decided that their three-legged race strategy of dragging the middle two legs and just runing with the outside legs worked for only one step. The ground was muddy where they fell, also. He hated being unnecessarily dirty. He was at that cool age, trying to impress girls with his biceps and crooked smile but still unsure of what he would do should one be charmed by his slicked-back hair.

My sister jabbed me repeatedly with her Barbie, the arms thrust out front like a swimmer. Every time I'd retaliate, my mother caught me. "Leave her alone."

It was summer; I was muddy and cold, sitting on a smelly blanket over the backseat hump of the Ford Fairlane. Sometimes being the middle child isn't all that great, so I thought about giant frogs eating cars like they were flies. Frogs only eat things that move, and we were moving. He'd spit me out, because I was a stinky mess. Right.

I guess that's when I started thinking about becoming a writer without knowing I was thinking about becoming a writer. I just didn't want to be stuck in the middle.

~~~~~

Doctor Visit

Today I have to get another two of those nasty basal carcinoma spots excised from my body. Six to nine stitches and we're done, but an unfamiliar doctor enters the room.

"Where's Dr. Jones?" I ask.

"She's unavailable," he says, his voice unemotional, his manner cold. No extended hand in greeting. No chitchat to comfort me, and I feel so in need of comfort in my backless gown and....

"Lie down."

I comply. He seems to know what he's doing. Goes directly to the spot on my arm and swabs it with the numbing agent. The spot on the leg is slightly bigger, and there's almost a grin on his face when he slathers it with the same agent. It seems generous and beyond anything I've had before. Then the needle comes out. It's a good sized needle, but nothing I haven't seen before.

"For pain," he says.

"Yeah, right," I jest. The pain is somewhat beyond the stinging of the needle for the purposes of numbing when he inserts it in my arm, then my leg. He sighs once he's done and then a slowly building laugh leaks out of his closed mouth.

"You don't remember me, do you?"

I look closer. "No."

The door bursts open. Two cops train their guns on him. He raises the needle with one hand and grabs me with the other. They shoot. The sound is deafening in the small room and the force of the blasts push him away from me as I struggle out of his grasp. He's resilient, and it takes two dozen shots or more before one cop reaches out and pulls me away. The needle falls to the floor. The man crumples. His blood flows.

Dr. Jones and even more police invade the small room. They hustle me out.

"Thank goodness we arrived in time," Dr. Jones says. "Be thankful he didn't prick you with the needle."

I start to shake. "But he did. Twice," I say. The pain in my leg and arm grows.

A look of horror comes across her face. The cops back away. Their guns now trained on me.

~~~~~

The Hand Job

"Hand!" Tiffany yelled.

"Where?" Mercedes asked, turning around several times in one place on her five-inch heels like a pencil rotating in a sharpener.

"There!" Tiffany pointed with her pink-tipped fingernail at the hand resting next to the bench outside the earring boutique and under a slender willow oak.

"Gross. And right here in Beverly Hills."

"Left or right?"

Mercedes' right hand hovered over the hand from the safe distance of three feet like a sorceress over a crystal ball. "Thumb to the left. Right. Ewww.

Right on...right on the ground."

"More like left off." Tiffany snapped her gum then giggled.

"Touch it."

"You."

"Scared?" Mercedes adjusted her micro-mini.

"Ut uh. But it's filthy."

"Go on. Ooo, use your umbrella."

Tiffany thought and thought and thought and thought and thought and thought and thought. "Okay." She extended the pink parasol but didn't open it. When she touched the palm of the hand, it closed tight around the umbrella.

She screamed. Mercedes screamed. Some effeminate guy across the street screamed, but did so because his car was being towed away. The umbrella flopped to the ground and the hand stuck to it like a wad of chewing gum from the Jolly Green Giant. Ho, ho, ho.

It didn't move.

They waited. Some guy in a Porsche whistled at them. They smiled back and yelled, "Hi ya," in unison.

The ignored hand grabbed Tiffany by the leg and swung her like a polo mallet knocking Mercedes under the wheels of a passing, well, Mercedes. She was officially dead now from the neck down. The hand dragged screaming Tiffany into the sewer grate.

An hour later, the first cop on the scene turned to the Detective, "Looks like another hand job."

"Get out your gloves," the detective said prophylactically, as he pulled back the grate.

"Wait. You can't go down there," said his lieutenant, looking up the street, past the gawking crowd.

"Someone has to rescue that girl," the detective argued.

"And that someone is coming."

The detective followed the lieutenant's gaze. "Is that...?"

"Yep."

He stepped back. "I thought he retired years ago."

"This is L.A., Hollywood, they all come back sooner or later. It's in their blood. And he is truly handy." The lieutenant gave a solid salute and then swept his arm down to his side. He pointed to the sewer. "They went that way."

Jumping into the sewer without hesitation, Thing, from The Addams Family fame was on the case.

~~~~~

Winning Without A Conscious

She showed up uninvited and almost ruined the party for me and everyone else. No one was sure whether she came alone or with someone. It was a moot point. She killed the buzz, deflated the enthusiasm, and sickened some people in the end. Her brown pixie haircut allowed her large almond-shaped eyes to dominate her face, making them seem even larger than they were – almost in a Spielberg take on aliens kind-of-way. The unblinking stare displayed two irises dark as an abyss. They were something you could get lost in, in a pleasurable way, while doing the horizontal tango. Her clothes matched her deep red lipstick: the simple mid-thigh evening dress, three-inch heels, and clutch purse. Her long nails, red, of course, clutched her sheer scarf like a lifeline.

In repose, she was a thing of beauty. In life, she was a screaming banshee mess, according to those who claimed to have met her previously. Dead, well, she made my party the talk of the town.

The party moved inside while the police did their investigation. In a way, the lieutenant's command, "No one leaves before I talk to each person," proved to be a joyous turn of events. The speculation over who killed her went viral. Someone posted pictures on YouTube. One of the cops even got drunk and was found by the lieutenant while making out with, Ginger, a *Victoria's Secret* model. The police have no sense of humor. They fired him. He married her the following week. She divorced him over Christmas. What a hoot.

Despite the initial buzz kill, the party turned out to be the year's hit event. Everyone claimed to have been there, although only thirty of us were present when Burt found her in the chaise lounge. The single, small caliber bullet hole at the base of her skull didn't even mess up her makeup. Her unsolved murder made prime time.

I wish she hadn't been such a complainer and had been more cooperative earlier that evening. She would have lived longer. I would have loved to have known her on a more personal level if you get my meaning.

That was two years ago, which is an eternity here in L.A. Things have slowed. I'm bored and staging a new party. There's a beautiful, but annoying redhead who's been dying to get into my pants and, no doubt, my wallet. Maybe I'll make one of her wishes come true. This time the outcome won't be unexpected. It's time to recreate the winning formula for another spectacular function. She will ruin the party, but the payback in publicity will be sublime.

I flipped open the phone and punched up Cheryl on speed dial. "Hello, Sweetie. I'm throwing a killer party next weekend."

~~~~~

The Pair

Two loud and obnoxious drunks dressed in suits and wearing throwback Indiana Jones hats walked down the damp street in front of me. The rain had washed away the pine pollen dust from the sidewalk, and it acquired a sheen as though it had been polished. The pollen floated atop the water, as it ran along the curbing, searching for gravity's well. Oak tree flowers and the propeller seeds from Maples had gathered along the streets, and in the level spots, water pooled behind the dam of nature's potential, gone to waste.

The drunks talked nonsense. The voices increased. They bumped hips like two aged fans of disco dancing. My date, a redhead of fine taste and finer body, squeezed my arm. I was sober, but she'd had a few. She giggled at their antics, though I was sure she didn't approve of the colorful language, being the lady that she was.

They stopped. We stopped twenty feet behind them.

"You laughing at me?" the shorter one said.

"Does it matter?" Red said.

"Let it go," the taller drunk said, laying a long arm around the broad, sloped shoulders of his shorter companion.

Shorty wasn't having any of it. "Off me." He turned to the taller man. They swatted at each other like limp-wristed cartoon characters whose game of patty-cake had turned violent.

Red laughed, and then snorted once. She covered her mouth, and even in the fuzzy grey of night, I saw

114

her face redden. Then, we both laughed.

The drunks stopped their slapping long enough to stare at us.

"Why I oughta." The short one charged. The tall one reached out and grabbed him by the shoulder. They lost their balance and swung their arms in wide circles, flapping the air for balance before grabbing each other and tumbling backwards into a large puddle on the street, breaking nature's dam, allowing the flow to continue, and the refuse of life to drain into the sewer.

We hurried forward partly out of concern, and partly because that was the way home. And for us, the evening was full of promise.

They were fine. The fall into the water and the realization of their situation had sparked a level of sobriety missing moments before.

Assured that no physical harm had come to them, Red said, "Goodnight, gentlemen." She added a shallow curtsey.

They doffed their hats and said, "Ma'am."

We strolled onward. She giggled, and then said, "Pair of nice boobs."

Two exhausting hours later, I lay in bed next to her. The rain fell outside, soothing as a lullaby. I laughed softly in the dark.

"What's so funny?" Red asked.

I pulled her toward me and kissed her breasts. "Pair of nice boobs," I said.

She giggled softly, and the sound lulled me to a blissful sleep.

~~~~~

On Writing

I tried writing in a coffee shop. Spilled coffee on the laptop and ruined it. When it shorted out, it caused an electrical fire to start smoldering in the wall of the old converted building, which was not up to the fire code.

Smoky flames burst through the wall next to the cappuccino maker after several minutes. The place had atmosphere with lots of wood contrasted with bright neon, ready fuel for a fire. During the panic to flee, several people were hurt. Some fat guy fell through the glass door unwilling to drop his $12.95 latte grandee with mocha diet coffee. He impaled himself on glass, cut his jugular, and bleed freely.

Other customers got sick at the sight. The smell soon became too much for some, and, well, you can guess what they did. The wall that was burning was common to the veterinary clinic next door. When smoke and flames started spewing forth, some snot-nosed high school girl with thick glasses, dressed in her charcoal-colored private school uniform took a broom and started yelling, "Free the animals."

So she did.

In the process, a rabid gray fox escaped and bit her. She cried and left the store. I know because she ran into my third cousin, two-times removed who had been at the coffee shop with me and bit him out of spite.

The coffee shop was an inferno by the time the firemen arrived. I left and stood down the street, watching the fox jump from person to person, biting with abandon.

The girl had lost her glasses. She was covered with soot. A car swerved to miss her on the smoky street and hit the fire hydrant. Water shot skyward, leaving the fire department without enough pressure to fight the fire. When the fox leapt at me, I was able to block it with the dead computer.

Stunned, it slunk into a corner, but still managed to bite the girl again when she came past him, soaking wet from the hydrant, her blouse plastered against her breasts, and showing more skin than a *Victoria Secret* model. I had to use the computer on her, too.

Two people applauded as she slumped to the ground, awake, but groggy. The fire spread. The soot got worse. I dragged the girl as I backpedaled away. Just then, the power to the area went out. All the bright neon gas leaked into the fire. Without water, the firemen sprayed ineffective foam that was quickly covered with ash from the smoldering fire. The flames, however, were still confined to the inside of the building, and masked by the roiling smoke.

In the oncoming twilight, the people, the fox, the buildings, and even the sky had turned fifty shades of gray. It was oddly beautiful. I was aroused. Even the girl started looking good. That is, except for the foaming mouth, blood from the bite marks, and the Dell tattoo on her forehead.

~~~~~

The Kiss

Dirk had me where he wanted me. High. My legs dangling. If he was quick enough, I would plop to the sand faster than the ice cream cone scoop I lost last week. My crotch would explode with pain moments after the hard wood hit, bounced up and.... It was too horrible to think about.

He smiled, seeing the fear in my eyes and worried look on my face. Not to mention my constant wiggling and glances downward.

"Don't do it," I said.

"Whatcha gonna do about it?" He slipped his muscular leg to one side, a tease.

"Dirk. Don't hurt Rick," Sally pleaded.

"Whatcha gonna do about it?"

Dirk sounded like my Grandma's one-note parrot before I dropped the bowling ball on it. Gawd, I could use the extra weight now to lift Dirk up. What I wouldn't give to weigh sixty pounds.

"I'll never speak to you again," Sally said, walking away from Dirk and toward me.

"Talking's overrated," Dirk replied. "At least that's what my old man says." He had one leg on the ground, and I felt my end of the seesaw dip. His shirt hung over the hand bar, but I knew his hands still held on tight. The taunting would continue until he got bored or his grammy would call him home.

"This can only end badly for you Dirk," I said.

"Whatcha gonna do about it?" He had called my bluff and leaned to shove off the seesaw, but Sally grabbed my side of it with unexpected speed and force. She hung on.

Dirk rose into the air, surprised by her sudden movement. His shirt caught on the hand bar as his body swung under the bar. He wrapped his legs around the seat and dangled upside down. I descended just slow enough that the feared crash never occurred. Our positions had been reversed.

"Let me down easy. Please," Dirk pleaded.

I slid to the end of the seat. "Whatcha gonna do about it?"

Sally let go. I jumped off. All seventy-five pounds of Dirk crashed to the ground and a great wailing erupted. I ran to Sally and like my father's favorite actor, John Wayne, had done to Maureen O'Hara, and like Elliott had done to the blond girl in "ET", I bent her backwards and kissed her long and hard, but not with the tongue as I heard my older brother talk about. That was gross.

Sally pushed me away. She swung hard and knocked me into the uncaring Dirk in the sand under the see-saw.

She wiped her hand across her face. "Ick. Boy germs." She ran away.

I wondered how long it would be before I got my second kiss. I liked the first one. I liked it a lot. I saw Mary Beth coming towards me with a concerned look on her face. Another of my dad's favorite movies crossed my mind. "Show me where it doesn't hurt."

~~~~~

Ugh!

"Ugh?" the cave man asked.

"Ugh. Ugh," his mate replied, pointing to her dull, lackluster brown hair that hung in tangled knots down to her hips.

He grabbed her by the hair, picked out the burrs, pieces of animal skin, and then sawed off most of her hair using his trusty flint arrowhead.

"Ugh." His mate said, pointing to the clump on the floor of their two-chambered cave.

"Ugh?" he responded.

"Ugh. Ugh," she replied, placing her arms akimbo.

He shrugged, grabbed the branch of a fir tree and thrust it into her hands. He pushed her to the mass of hair. She swept the cave floor. Done. She squashed the raspberries in the bowl he had made of a tree that did not rot. He grabbed his mate by her hair.

"Ugh? Ugh. Ugh!" she said. He bent her over backwards, and then smooshed her ragged mane into the goop in the bowl. He kept her there. He laughed. Soon, she started to massage her own head in the goop. He let go, sensing she was enjoying his actions.

"Ugh." She pointed. He threw the squirrel skins at her. She wrapped her head in them. He left.

Hours later, after a successful Mastodon hunt and a satisfying romp through the warm springs, he returned to the cave. The squirrel skins hung near the entrance. The grayish pelts were a ruined mass of red. He was not pleased. "Ugh!" The sound echoed from the cave into the forest.

Furious, he walked into the rear chamber of the

cave where the setting sun angled into the normally dark interior as a shaft of brilliant light. She stood arms clasped behind her, her red hair straightened by her fishbone comb, a touch of the raspberry juice highlighting her pouty lips. She had also been to the warm springs. The mud flats smell was gone and replaced by the musk of yesterday's mink. A white flower, growing on a vine that invaded the cave through a crack in the wall, stuck in her hair when she backed up. He stared at her, dressed in a lion skin that covered little.

His senses exploded: her, the flower, the new look of red hair framing her porcelain face, the ruby lips and the way they tasted as they thrashed on the bed of soft down he'd had collected for them from a flock of geese when they'd first met. One of the hay-stuffed animal pouches they used for a pillow burst about the same time they had finished the conquest of each other's loins.

They panted in the debris of their lust. She noticed the hay and handed him the tree branch.

"Ugh." She pointed to the mess on the cave floor.

He looked at her with a furrowed brow. "Ugh, ugh!"

She turned away from him. Seconds later, she looked at him with eyes half closed and lips blazoned red again.

"Ugh." She pointed to the mess on the floor. "Ugh, ugh." Her hands cupped her breasts.

He swept up the mess.

History was over; the rest is herstory.

~~~~~

The Rant to Respectability

Four days! I've been at the screen for four days. My fish in the aquarium are dead. The birds are alive only because I had forgotten to close the door to their cage. They have nibbled on the crumbs from my meals found in dark corners of the refrigerator, freezer, or pantry. I don't remember any of them. The cockatiel even tried the baked chicken leg. Little cannibal. My shirt stank after the first two days; my underwear reeked after three. I don't have time for laundry, let alone to separate the whites from the darks, the stay-fast from the wash-and-wear.

Naked, I worry about nothing, but the screen in front of me, and the words I write to fill it.

I'm no longer even paranoid about the monkey on the fire escape looking in on me. I know he's for real. He wants to eat my brains. But the deadline is looming, and currently, if you don't publish a new novel every other week, someone else will. It is do or die, and that's not a joke any longer. Those of us who write are at the mercy of those who read. They want more; they want it faster; they demand it more exciting. There is no time to be witty, polishing words with subtext, subliminal messages, and obscure references that only the intelligentsia might understand. "Night on Bald Mountain" is not a fancy composition. It is someone having sex with a large bald man while planning his demise with a Mentos and diet cola bomb shoved...well, you get the point.

The body has to hit the floor on page two. Lovers have to always unite at the end---she with her large bosom in a dress too small for Dolly Parton and him with his throbbing manhood that wouldn't fit in a pantaloon. No prologues, except for sci-fi and fantasy so you can explain this wondrous world you've built, so you can give all these creatures the same mannerisms, thoughts, actions, and moralities of people in our own world. Why? If you're going to invent a new world, make sure the goal of word makers is to eat the young of agents, publishers, and marketers to free the word makers from bondage.

There, I've put onto paper the unthinkable, that we, the word makers, are slowly becoming the enemy of ourselves. We must write, edit, produce, create artwork, summarize, categorize, slot, and market our words. We must group those words into appropriately-slotted sizes and genres, scrounge for reviews, blurbs, conferences, workshops, readings, and other venues in which to present our words to meager audiences who will pay only $.99 for anything we write. And yet, we continue to write more. We have become the agents of our own demise.

Heavy footfalls resound up the stairs. I hear them coming. They tromp up five flights because the elevator is broken. Let them wheeze their way here. I continue to type. I'm well passed the 60,000 barrier for a romance novel. It's too wordy. I know it, but can't help myself. No one will slot it on the shelf. It won't get face time on the end of the aisle.

They are at the door. They're polite. I give them that. They bang on the door, "Book Police. We have a warrant."

"So nice of you to knock. Go away."

One smashes through the window, and I cast an old *Funk and Wagnall's* dictionary at him. He responds with an unabridged thesaurus. It grazes my arm. The door comes down, and they rush in shouting strong verbs and muttering adjectives. I can't write any more, and am better for it. The release is mine; the loss is theirs. They turn off my spellchecker and close down my computer

Justice is swift. Two days later in the stark white courtroom filled with dozens of people glued to their screens, the screen in front of me flashes my crime: low sales.

The next day, I'm cast from mid-list into the oblivion of self-publishing Hell. I have to fight my way through the throngs of wannabes, could have been's, might still be's. I'm looking for the right combination of words to float onto paper and be transported to writing Heaven with a contract worthy of my words and nine months between releases and a scheduled book tour and an advance with which to buy bird food. I find a turnip in the grocery store while shopping for ideas. I pick it up.

"As God is my witness, I shall never go wordy again."

~~~~~

Cicadacide

At some point, Bob Zucker slept. At another point, he awoke, but as he lay there in bed, he couldn't recall either of those points in time or how long they had lasted. All he could think about was the damn noise the cicadas made. Hour after hour, day after day, night after night. And he left the noise of the city for the peacefulness of the country. He turned over in bed and realigned his pillow over his ears. "I could sleep better under the El."

The cicadas seemed to be pointing their unwanted attentions at him. For the first three weeks, he heard them everywhere: home, work, at the park, fishing, outside the bowling alley, coming home drunk from the bar. "Ubiquitous." The word dribbled out of his mouth, as he slipped out of bed and went to the kitchen for a beer and whiskey chaser. The sleeping pill wasn't working. He could feel tightness in his chest. He belched. Some relief. He noticed the cicada noise was a bit less intense in the kitchen, so he drank there.

He cursed the cicadas. He cursed his boss, Mr. Barrister, for the pressure the bastard applied when he knew that Bob was having trouble sleeping. He cursed Acme HVAC for not fixing his air conditioning unit, and then not returning when he'd threatened them with a lawsuit. He cursed his wife, Matilda, for insisting on the move out to the country, and then for leaving him just after the cicadas started their racket. She claimed it was his temper, not the bugs. Everyone and everything else can dump on him, but he's not supposed to get angry about it? Right!

125

One beer became two. Two led to a third with another shot.

By the fourth one, he envisioned the death of each cicada. "Damn their crusty little empty-shelled bodies everywhere." When he had opened the fifth beer and drank the third shot, he got up and staggered over to the gun case. He extracted the shotgun, and then decided on his deer rifle. "More noise for the little buggers to deal with."

Out on the porch, he loaded four shells. He fired at the tall oak in front of the house. "Take that you bastards." His neighbor's light came on and a voice rang out.

"Bob, are you nuts? Put that gun away before you hurt someone."

"Screw you, Mark."

Bob fired again and then laughed before noticing that the noise seemed to have diminished somewhat. "Hey, maybe the little buggers don't like loud noises." He fired a third shot higher in the tree. "Maybe there's more of you up there."

"Bob, put the gun down." Mark marched up Bob's driveway. His wife, Abigail, trailed behind him.

Bob sneered. "Can't you see I'm trying to help everyone out?"

"Mark, don't go there," Abigail pleaded, tugging on his shirt tail.

"Just leave this to me," he hissed back at his wife.

"He's drunk again. Let it go."

Bob laughed. Mark stepped onto the sidewalk leading up to the front porch. Bob's demeanor changed. He pointed the gun at Mark. "Get the heck off my property."

"Don't be stupid and don't point that gun at

me."

"I'll point it anywhere I want."

Abigail stepped in front of Mark. "Let's just go."

"Yeah, go." Bob echoed Abigail's request.

Mark stared at Bob. With Abigail pulling on his arm, Mark finally turned and walked away.

Another shot rang out. Abigail screamed. Mark grabbed her. They both turned around to see Bob laughing, his rifle on his hip pointing to the sky. "Cicadas got you spooked?" Bob said, and then stuck out his tongue at the two of them before he dropped to the ground.

Later, Detective Stark examined Bob's prone body. "This is another one for that website about dumb people doing dumb things," Stark said. "First he shoots at the tree, then he confronts his neighbor, then he fires one shot straight into the air, and damn if it doesn't come right down on him catching the artery just right. He bled out in four minutes."

"Stupid bastard," the patrol officer said. "Found the source of that noise. This white noise generator is set to turn on every night at nine. It was in the attic, but whoever put it there forgot to unplug it. Damn thing sounds like cicadas."

"Yep, glad that racket's over with for another seven years," Stark said, turning the noise generator around. "Says here, it's the property of Maltida Zucker. She must be his wife."

~~~~~

Summer Reading Program

I continue to plow through self-published or faux self-published books. I put up reviews on the blog every Wednesday. I want to read more novels; I want to read more polished novels. Most of the self-published writers have good story ideas, but fail to realize the full potential of those ideas.

However, writing really takes a toll on reading, as does the extensive gardening I do. Family also takes up too much time, also. I married into a large family. There are fifty-nine direct descendants from my mother- and father-in-law's and counting. They have, at least, one "emergency" every thirty-six hours. And being an available writer at-home, in other words, an unemployed person, I should learn to screen my calls better to prevent being dragged into those emergencies.

"Well, you're not doing anything are you?" my brother-in-law says when he calls me up.

"Well, yes I am. I'm reading."

"That's not as important as the hanging toenail I have. Those things can really hurt. You're the only one who clips toenails with such precision."

"It comes from cutting coupons out of the newspaper so I don't starve. I have lots of practice."

"Oh, you're so funny."

I missed the humorous part and trudge across town to his house.

"Oh my God! I've seen bears in the wild with better maintained toes. We have to get you to a doctor immediately."

Seven hours later, the battery on my kindle has

long since died. The guy with the arrow through his mid-section can still only lie on his side. His elbow is propped up on a fat book as he stares at me with hatred while doctors in some remote corner of the hospital mull over what to do about his situation. The woman nearest him hasn't moved in four hours; she may be dead. I hear a saw every now and then. I wonder if it's related to my in-law's toenail issue; those things were massive.

It's 2 a.m. I'm bored out of my skull. There isn't even a pretty nurse to ogle. Two other relatives came and went hours ago. "We have work in the morning. You can write any time."

I've been through the twenty newsstand entertainment and information (joke here) magazines. It takes only four minutes each, and that includes reading the articles. I always have and still think Zooey Deushell is the hottest woman out of all the twigs draped with cloth between the pages. And it's amazing how much there is to say or photograph about the same person in each publication. And just who is Inga Jellyfish? Is her story for real?

The first drunk spills through the door. The bars have closed. An orderly mops him up and squeegees him onto a chair. Two more drunks come in; one has a black eye that's bleeding. Drunk Number 2 is the happy kind, laughing and joking with the no-nonsense Admission's Clerk. However, when #2 sees Arrowman, he gets real quiet.

"I saw dat 'afore." He walks toward Arrowman, who gets a look of concern.

Just then, an orderly whisks my brother-in-law through the door in a wheelchair. He scoops up Bleeding Eye and exits back through the same door.

Dead Woman sucks in a breath. #2 hovers over Arrowman. The two doctors who looked at Arrowman hours ago return. My brother-in-law says, "What are you waiting for? Let's go."

#2 yells, "Son of Cochise. In the movie, they had to remove an arrow."

#2 grabs the arrow on the backside of Arrowman. Arrowman screams, "What the freak do you think you're doing, you butthole?" The doctors run toward Arrowman. My in-law screams, because he's a screamer. #2 snaps the arrow in half. As the pointy end drops to the floor, he reaches around Arrowman and pulls out the shaft from the front, holding it aloft like an Olympic gold medal.

"Mother of God," screams Arrowman. He rises and socks #2 in the face. #2 hits Dead Woman with a flailing arm, waking her up. He then falls backwards into my brother-in-law. The jagged edge of the arrow sticks into my brother-in-law's fleshy thigh. He screams. An orderly grabs #2 and holds him down. The doctors sprint to Arrowman, who's up and holding a bloody shirt to the front hole.

"Man. That feels a lot better. This was quicker and cheaper than you yahoos," he says to the doctors. He heads to the door, trailing drops of blood across the waiting room.

The doctors beg him to stay. He refuses.

A rent-a-cop takes away #2. Dead Woman is asleep again. The doctors take my brother-in-law to deal with the new wound.

My brother-in-law stops screaming and yells, "You should have learned more about cutting toenails."

They whisk him away, but still I hear him wail,

"This is your entire fault, you bum." Then comes one more plaintive plea from down the corridor. "Wait for me."

Seems that I'm always a bum as long as writing is my job and a self-published writer, and waiting for my turn on the New York Times best-sellers list. It also makes me available for everyone else to claim their unwavering confidence in me after the fact. But all is not lost; Arrowman had been leaning on "War and Peace". Finally, I have something to read. My summer reading program is not all lost yet.

~~~~~

On Pleasing Everybody

I sweated in the unforgiving wooden kitchen chair. I usually talk with my hands, but couldn't at the moment. That made me nervous, and once I start talking, I tend to blabber, giving up my thoughts and ideas without understanding what I've done.

She sat in a deep, high-back soft chair, the kind when viewed from the profile, you might not notice anyone sitting there, obscured by the wings of the chair.

She was a throwback. Her suit, shoes, hair style, and even the hat she wore were from some 1940s Hollywood storage closet. She had a nice face though, but she kept it hidden. It was as though if I knew the details of face, the lines and curves, the exact color of her eyes, the shape of her ears; or the imperfections, the tiny scar from a dog bite, where an angry zit left a too-deep mark, that one eyebrow had a tiny gap in continuity that had to be filled in; that knowing these things might give me some power over her.

The overhead lamp glowed brightly, but the hat threw a shadow that eclipsed her face. Only her cherry lips and dimpled chin were in full light. The rest of her rested in the shadows, along with the reasons she was pumping me for information.

She pulled out a cigarette and lit it. "Go on with this problem of pleasing everybody."

"Okay. Well. Getting everything right for every reader is a problem. In fact, it has inspired me to write another story about a frustrated writer who travels to the Caribbean on vacation after receiving yet another rejection from a targeted agent who blasts the literary aspects of his novel. While in the Caribbean, the writer runs into his greatest nemesis, the woman who told him to write in those changes that infuriated the agent. He plots revenge.

"He musters the nerve to kill her, and then frames her live-in boyfriend for her murder. However, he can't leave because a hurricane hits the island, grounds the planes, and destroys the jail. That frees the boyfriend, who knows the truth about his girlfriend's murder.

"Morally unable to kill the writer, the boyfriend seduces a local voodoo-woman, a high priestess, who is a voracious reader and hates poorly written books. He promises to be her lover if she raises his dead girlfriend as a zombie to kill the writer.

"The writer waits in a shabby motel full of trapped Portuguese vacationers. But when the writer meets up with the zombized girlfriend, who's mumbling, "Brains," in a German-Spanish accent, a confused Portuguese Water Dog thinks she said, "Bacon," and jumps on the fragile zombie-girl, killing her, and eating what's left of her brains in the process out of hunger. Of course, this turns the dog into a zombie.

"After terrorizing the trapped tourists, the zombie dog is finally put down. The writer sweats out another long day's delay, fearful the police are on to him. However, when the writer finally flies out, he's upgraded to first class because of the delay. A drunk and flirtatious Katy Perry settles into the seat next to him on the connecting flight out of Miami.

"She finds him charming and invites him to stay with her in New York City when they land, because her new boyfriend is a boring elitist snob. They land

133

and catch a cab. They kanoodle in the cab as the writer anticipates a free weekend of Katy-love. As they arrive at the hotel, a man opens the cab's door. It's the agent who had rejected the writer. The agent is also Katy's boyfriend. The agent and the new writer boyfriend get into an argument on the sidewalk. The agent kills the writer. That's one of the big twists.

"The agent dies before going to trial. The writer's estate finds an agent for the book. It becomes a mega-bestseller, selling 70,000,000 copies in a year, more than Dan Brown's *The DaVinci Code*.

"Exonerated from the murder of his girlfriend, the island girl's boyfriend sues for some of the royalties on behalf of her and her input, which he now claims mostly came from him. He wins $22,567,342.82.

"He meets Katy Perry at the trial. They fall in love, but the girlfriend is raised from the dead one last time. Death by canine is against rule 7.23.4 in the Voodoo Handbook, and she hadn't fulfilled the murderous portion of her unholy contract even though the writer is now dead.

"Zombie-girl accidentally kills her boyfriend by collapsing in pieces on him, sticking a rib through his rib cage into his heart while he and Katy were making love. Katy freaks and joins a convent. The voodoo-woman rejoices over her revenge because the boyfriend had pladged eternal love to her in the first place.

"The story ends with her hatching a plan to raise her former lover, the agent. Though he hated the author's book as much as she did, he needs to pay for leaving her and taking up with Katy.

"All this proves is that no book pleases everyone

and sometimes the editing consequences can be deadly."

I'm sweating buckets now. She lights up another cigarette and blows smoke in my direction. She coughs. It's dainty and faint. With no fanfare, she rises and walks toward the door. "Try again and no freaking zombies." She fades away before she reaches the doorknob. She is gone.

I am alone. "Muse. Come back."

~~~~~

The Great Escape

The alarm sounds at 5:30 a.m. I notice that the ISP server rejected all the emails sent last night. It happens about once a year. I resend. I discover that the sprinkler I had turned on in the dark before dealing with the emails has tipped over. Practical joke by a deer, I assume, so I reset it. In the twilight of morning, I step on a snake while entering the garden. Luckily it's non-poisonous and only strikes my sneaker before slithering off. I return with about a pound of okra, ten big tomatoes, sixty-four cherry and grape tomatoes, four cucumbers, two green peppers, two Jalapeno peppers, and a tick crawling up my arm.

I burn the tick and wash the veggies, before I notice that one of the hummingbird feeders is missing. I look down at the edge of the pond expecting to see it shattered amongst the rocks. Phew! It's intact, but to string another wire is a difficult process that will take fifteen minutes.

My wife has been promising all summer to weed the area around the pond. Now, that task is mine so I can retrieve the fallen hummingbird feeder. Fifteen minutes later, it is hung. Angry hummers feed immediately. No thanks. No gentle fanning of my beaded brow.

I remove the second tick of the morning and enjoy his fiery death. Nightfall came before I could finish weed whacking last evening, so I grab the whacker, and after ten seconds, a hidden wire has wrapped itself around the rotating shaft. I'll save it for the afternoon to fix in the garage when it's too hot to

136

work outside.

Heading back into the garage, I notice the tire on my wife's car is flat. Another deer joke? No. More likely the handiwork of squirrels. I'll deal with it after I take down a dead tree that is liable to fall on the house should we get the potential storm, Gabrielle, this weekend. Two-thirds through the cut, the chain saw stops working. It has gas and lubricating oil, but won't kick over. I change the plug. Something's wrong. I load it into the back of the car to take it to the repair shop in the middle of the woods (story for another day).

I'm sweaty. I'm frustrated. I need breakfast. Sydney, my twenty-year-old cockatiel wants attention. He alights on my shoulder.

"Whatchadoing?" he asks.

I tell him. He doesn't care and picks at his feathers. As I'm flipping the bacon, the alarm sounds that the water needs to be shut off. I pass through the garage and open the back door as I've done a thousand times before. The water spigot is right there. Sydney gets spooked by something unseen by human eyes and screams bloody murder.

His wings are clipped so he can't fly. He's flopped off me before outside. Ten to fifteen feet later, he always plops to the ground, looks back at me, and alarmingly runs toward me as if to suggest, "What in the heck am I doing on the ground?"

This time, he makes it to the balloon flowers. That's impressive. Suddenly, he has lift. Down the driveway he goes gaining height. 150 feet later at the end of the driveway, he makes a right turn as if he knows where he's going, and I'm in hot pursuit in my stocking feet.

By the time I reach the end of the driveway, he's nowhere to be seen. I call. No response. I run down the road a hundred feet. No response to my continued calls. I rush back to the house, turn off the water, and enter.

The bacon is smoking up the house and the smoke detector sounds a deafening roar. (At least I know it works.) I turn off the burner, flip the bacon onto the paper towel, and dump the grease into a can. The frying pan is tossed into the sink under a dash of cold water. I lace up my sneakers to the sound guaranteed to attract the attention of the police and neighbors and roving bands of bandits. Unfortunately, I live in the middle of the woods on a cul-de-sac with only five lots and four houses, and no neighbors home during the day, I'm alone in my search for Sydney during his great escape.

I run up the road in the direction in which he flew, which is toward the end of the cul-de-sac. I try to think like a bird. (Pause for you to think of all your bird brain jokes.) I figure that since he's never flown in the woods before, he won't go beyond the yard of the last house on the street. The thick woods would seem like a daunting place for a twenty-year-old bird to be flying who believes he's just a small person. I just hope their dog is inside. He's friendly to me, but Sydney might look like a doggie treat.

I call for Sydney. No reply. I whistle. No reply. I'm on their driveway heading for the back of their property when I yell, "Sydney," once more. I hear a faint chirp. Yes, there are many birds in our little oasis. I feed hundreds of them a day. I may not know all their calls or be able to tell which call belongs to which bird, but like a father in a crowded shopping mall with hundreds of screaming kids, I know the sound of my own.

I call again. No reply.

I change tactics. Sydney has a small repertoire of words or phrases he knows, maybe twenty of them, twelve of which even non-bird parents can understand.

"Peek a boo," I call.

"Peek a boo," he shouts back from my right, somewhere in the woods. Oh, please don't be up a tree. He'll want me to come to him, and I'm not Tarzan. There are no vines. I call again.

He answers me, "Peek a boo." I get a fix on where he's at. We repeat the process five more times before he goes silent. I try a different call to keep him interested in this life or death game. Snakes, dogs, ticks, lice, coyotes, fox, and any other of a number of predators could be homing in on his troubled calls.

"Jack and Joy," I call. He responds immediately. I'm getting close, but I know he'll only do this call a couple of times. I try again. He responds. Again, and he goes silent. I call his name. Nothing. For the first time, I'm really worried.

I call his name over and over again, not moving in the woods so I can hear his response. Nothing. MY WIFE IS GOING TO KILL ME. I may have to move to rural Maine to hide from her. Finally, I try, "Peek a boo," one more time. Leaves rattle at my feet. He looks up at me from under a fallen twig still clutching its leaves.

"Peek a boo."

Stupid bird. Now isn't the time for games. I'd been standing next to him for the last three minutes. Relieved, I pick him up and carry him home. I put him on the short counter top where he lives, and he heads for his box (he prefers a box) and from inside the box, he sticks his head out.

"Peek a boo."

He seems relieved to be in his comfort zone and assumes a napping position. It's 9:16 a.m. I'm stressed, but my day is improving. My child is home and safe.

~~~~~

Finding Inspiration

After leaving the service and armed with the G.I. bill, I lived in a small college town for four years while pursuing my English degree. I had selected a creative writing course for the fall term. Wanting to get a head start on my coursework, I decided to write a few short stories during a three-week period between the end of summer session and the beginning of the fall term.

Splat. Brain freeze. I needed to do something radical to jumpstart the old synapses.

Over breakfast in a local diner the next morning, I heard someone lament, "The most exciting thing in this town is watching the light change."

Yes, it's a cliché, and we did have only one light at the junction of the two two-lane highways, and when school was out, there wasn't much to do in a dry town in a dry county in which there are more deer than people, and bears often roamed the edge of town looking for garbage can delights. I decided to test the theory. I would spend 24 hours watching the light change and decide for myself if it is truly is the most exciting thing happening in this town.

I reasoned it would be best to start in the late afternoon after rising at noon, which was normal for me in the summer. I watched the light cycle from green to orange to red from my post on the only downtown sidewalk bench. I figured having my own chair might be too provocative.

The local deputy harassed me several times. He even tried to arrest me for being a vagrant. He couldn't. I had more than five dollars on me, and I wasn't homeless; I had mail from my Post Office box and an electric bill for my address on me to prove residency. Until then, I never knew there was a threshold for being a vagrant.

"I'm not happy about this," he said. "You're up to no good."

Three young ladies propositioned me around eleven that night. Only the anemic blonde in the cutoff jeans and sparkly blouse was remotely tempting and seemingly legitimate with her suggestion. She hung with me for about fifteen minutes, absorbing my body warmth on the bench when I noticed her shivering. I offered her my jacket; she preferred another stick of gum. A gust of wind came up, and she blew away to another port in the night. The other two probably would have passed out or been sick before we got anywhere to do anything. A dry town in a dry county doesn't mean there wasn't alcohol around.

Four different people threw items at me during the night: a *Budweiser* beer can, empty cup of coffee, wad of paper with nothing written on it, and a light bulb that shattered in the gutter. Maybe someone was trying to "turn on the light" for me. Later, someone said that they were probably trying to turn out my lights. Both might have been true.

The deputy rolled by while I picked up most of the shards from the broken light bulb. "Cleaning up my home," I said. He glared. Humor was not his strong suit.

Northern Pennsylvania in mid-August in the middle of the night is colder than you might think. I wore a sweat suit emblazoned with my college's name – Mansfield State College. It seemed that it would be the most comfortable choice of clothing. I had my jacket that Blondie didn't want to crawl into. And in my backpack, I had gloves and a knit hat. Unfortunately, my college's colors were red and black. When I put on the knit hat and gloves, I disappeared into the shadows like a Ninja warrior. Of course, that was the moment when Deputy Fife happened by again.

"I've got my eyes on you," he yelled from the car, looking about ten feet to my right.

The dead of night is not midnight. It is 3:30 a.m. At that time of the night, all the drunks have made it home or have driven off the sides of the mountains, and the early-bird workers haven't hit the streets yet. The crickets have ceased their racket; bugs have snuggled somewhere; the bats have given up chasing the bugs; people, smart ones, are nestled in warm beds with open windows, accepting the cool night air into their lives. The streetlights are out by then. Even the yappy dogs have ceased barking, having declared their territory against real and imaginary foes in the dark.

It's lovely, dark, and urban deep. It's beautiful in its own way.

Excitement? I saw two fender-benders and lots of trucks at night. I was surprised by how many rolled by: at least one every ten minutes. A Model-T appeared from the short-lived morning fog like an apparition, and then puttered away. Two Corvettes—both yellow—roared through town; various people sat with me, but none for more than an hour; some woman, very concerned about my mental state, tempted me with chocolate-chip cookies if I would come into the small downtown clinic for a chat. I was able to snatch two cookies without going in.

Animals are about more than we realize. I saw plenty of the usual suspects. At 4 a.m., a deer jaywalked from behind a closed frat house, crossed the highway, and wandered through the Mr. Donuts parking lot without pausing to look both ways. Where was the deputy then? She stood by a dumpster for a few minutes. Disgusted that there were no leftovers, she kicked the refuse container and left. I don't believe she ever saw me.

A fresh-faced, female townie, sporting sparkly green eyes and red hair to match mine, thought that what I was doing was bold, cool, daring, and even far out. "You deserve a prize," she said, before leaving for her two-day-a-week job waiting tables at the nicest restaurant in town. I waved goodbye as she slipped into the Gaslight shortly before ten in the morning.

Tick-tock. Four p.m. rolled around without fanfare. Was watching the light change in town the most exciting thing? I wasn't sure. There was a blinking light at the edge of town I hadn't thought about until someone mentioned it around noon. Could that be more exciting?

I left my post and bowed in all four compass directions to no one in particular. I walked home intent on making a nice home-cooked meal in celebration of my dubious achievement. As I turned the corner to my hole-in-the-wall apartment above the dry cleaners, the nubile townie came towards me, wearing a smile, tank-top, and a jean skirt shorter than most two-piece bathing suits. I stopped and waited for her to cover the few yards between us. When she came up to me, she kissed me on the cheek and took my hand, leading me to my apartment.

"Name's Gail."

"I'm Rick."

"I know." She'd done her homework.

Gail helped me engage in some horizontal admiration for my efforts over the next few hours. The bonus included a free pizza, delivered, eaten in bed, and drowned with the only two beers I had. She left like Cinderella, fleeing just as midnight chimed in the apartment. I had relieved her summertime boredom; she had thawed my writing brain freeze. I slumbered like a bear in hibernation.

The next few evenings turned out to be exceptionally exciting, and I did learn one thing: watching the light change in my small college town wasn't the most exciting thing around. Just wish she'd been a year older, and that her brother wasn't the deputy that found out about us.

Excitement cranked up after that.

~~~~~

The View

Tiffany Bouvier could not recall the previous fifteen minutes of her life. Those minutes were gone. She stared at the clock on her computer to reassure herself that time had passed. The clock didn't lie. Her first reaction was to consider alien abduction, but she didn't feel as she'd had the last time that happened. She shook her body to awaken herself. She realized that she had just spaced out, allowed herself to function on automatic pilot no different from someone driving the same route to work every day, arriving, and not remembering a single detail about the trip.

"Four days," she mumbled. "Haven't slept in four days, because I know that guy at that construction site across the street is watching me. Leering. Lusting." She sighed. "I could use a bit of lusting."

She slammed her hand on the desk. "I am not paranoid." She pressed her palms together to calm herself. Then, she sipped a warm diet cola, another soldier for the stack against the wall. She stood and placed the empty can on top of the column of cans next to all the neatly stacked columns that nearly filled her office. Her office was really just a partitioned portion of the over-sized bedroom that dominated her older apartment, built long before the cookie-cutter designs that now inundated the city. "Ninety-nine bottles of beer on the wall, my ass," she said, and then chuckled. "Look at it. Must be 100,000 cans stacked perfectly." She knew exactly how many cans, but liked round numbers. Still, she couldn't help but

146

mumble the truth, "Ninety-nine thousand, nine-hundred, and seventy-eight." For over thirty years, she'd collected her babies, sometimes her only friends, and early-on, her playmates. So many cans filled the room that when the light shined just right, the office had a dull reddish hue.

A soft breeze edged its way under a window open only wide enough for a dream to slip or a nightmare to escape. Now, the seepage of construction sounds was enough to return her focus to the building site. Tiffany sat back down. "Look. I told you I'm not crazy. He's looking right at me." Tiffany sat as still as a mouse hiding in the shadow of a hawk. A gray business suit draped the man like a knight's armor. His yellow hardhat, adorned with streaks of silver, covered his head like a helmet. He stood behind the construction barriers, acting as ramparts; the street a moat. "Handsome man," she said, and watched and waited. "What? No snappy response?" She clucked her tongue several times.

When he pointed in her direction, like a knight signaling his intent, her heart pounded. Tiffany grabbed her comb. She combed her hair, making sure each strand fell into place. Her clothes weren't presentable, and she pushed away from the computer intent on changing them, but then he turned away and vanished into the belly of the building being erected. Exhausted, she lay her head on the table feeling rejected. "Don't mock me," she lamented.

#

Tiffany awoke with a start. She listened intently for sounds beyond her racing heartbeat. The city's steady hum still leaked into the room from the darkened night, seeking companionship with her computer's hum and soft twilight glow. The slow monotonous drip from her kitchen sink matched the lonely flashing of a neon sign. A mouse or rat scurrying somewhere in the apartment wall signaled desperation. However, as her senses sharpened, she realized the plain truth. No one had broken in. No one had called her. No one needed her. She'd just woken up from a dead sleep to an empty day.

She moved her computer's mouse and the rolling wave screensaver lit up and answered her unasked question. "Four a.m. Monday?" She'd been asleep since sometime late Saturday afternoon. Her vacation was over. No man magically knocked on her door. No great adventure happened. She won at online Texas Draw. She lost most of it with bets on the ponies. Work beckoned. A caffeine withdrawal headache pounded, and she ached from her awkward sleeping position. She had peed on her chair. "Life sucks."

#

Tiffany entered her apartment at two in the afternoon after eight hours at the bakery. In the back room of the bakery, she talked to no one while preparing materials for the bakers and stacking supplies others had unloaded from delivery trucks. The bakers jabbered endlessly with each other and a stream of customers she never saw from her tomb-like work place. She was a reliable fixture, an invisible automaton who had never missed a day of work.

She had forgotten to eat again and hunger clawed at her insides. She cooked a small steak and ate it with peas and a sweet potato in front of the kitchen sink, listening to some second-rate, right-wing fill-in talk show commentator go on about the death of civility brought on by the liberals in society. She wondered for a fleeting moment if the commentators really believed the opinions they spewed or whether it was all hype for money. She didn't care. Civility didn't seem to exist.

The appeal of the bakery's doughnuts and breads had ended years ago. Her weight had retreated over time until she was almost as slender as she had been at fourteen when she had to take the job, times being what they were, and events unfolding as they did. At thirty-nine, the only difference was that she was slightly taller, much stronger, and even lonelier than the child she was back then. No friends would call on her, and she would mature in isolation to become a young woman with no suitors, and finally, no family.

Tiffany's shower promised no impassioned lover's embrace as she let the flour residue rinse off. Molasses had dribbled onto her ankle. She took care to get every sticky spot off, and then, to ensure she had washed off the bakery, she used a fragrant body lotion sampler that came in the mail. It made her feel somewhat elegant; so on went the red, silk pajamas that she saved for Christmas. "In for a penny, in for a dollar," she announced, applying the meager portions of makeup she'd accumulated from other samplers over the years. "Like it?" she asked. No response. "The pajamas require a sash." She tied a bright blue sheer scarf around her waist, pulling it tight, positioning it so as to amplify the curves of her body.

Satisfied, she sat down at her computer, flicked it on, and brushed her hair. As it powered up, she kept an eye on the construction site. Men did what men did, but her knight was not there. She played solitaire for several minutes before the doorbell rang.

Tiffany closed her office door as she went to answer the doorbell. Through the peephole, she saw the man she had seen from across the street, her knight. A rush of sexual arousal enveloped her, catching her off guard with its intensity. The very fact that it erupted so fast and so easily excited her beyond measure. It pleased and embarrassed her. She stared at him through the peephole, awed by his presence.

He smiled, realizing she was spying on him when she had moved the peephole cover. She opened the door a crack. "Hi," he said.

"Can I help you?" Tiffany squeaked out each word, as her lustful urges grew nearly beyond her control.

"Can I come in and talk to you?"

No one ever came to her door, not even the building manager. Neighbors never bothered her, and now there seemed to be fewer and fewer of them all the time. She managed her own repairs, painted when necessary, and never complained. Her hands shook as she unlatched the lock and opened the door in slow hesitant increments. He took her hand and shook it. She didn't know whether to scream or climax. He held on to her hand as though he was salvation itself and her hand a prize worth winning.

"I'm Michael D'Anglo. I'm the architect for the building across the street." His radiant smile nearly pushed her aside, as he gently made his way into her miniscule foyer, gently brushing against her. He scanned the kitchen and dining room areas as he continued to talk. "Surprisingly spacious," he said and then continued. "My company has been interested in renovating this neighborhood for quite some time."

She wished she had cleaned up after her meager

meal. She could feel the rush of blood to her face over her embarrassment. It only added to the warmth she was already feeling.

He kept holding her hand like a lover would, but reached behind with the other one and closed the apartment door for her and latched it. Their stance was almost an embrace. Tiffany's knees nearly betrayed her. He was more handsome up close than what she could see from peering at him from across the street. At six feet, he was almost a foot taller than her. His presence and strong cologne seemed to fill the room. With the door closed now, she felt in awe of him in that tight space. "I'm sorry. I didn't catch that."

"I said we've bought most of the apartments in this building." He paused. "I was going to let the lawyers handle negotiations with you, but I was intrigued by the red glow in your window, I suspect your bedroom, and had to check it out for myself. It's very artistic in nature and architecturally captivating." His smile became lopsided as though he wanted to put his dimple on display. He nodded his head in the direction of her interior door. Tiffany shook her head.

"I was told a beautiful woman lived here alone. I wasn't misinformed. Was I?"

Tiffany shook her head to indicate no, and then nodded her head overwhelmed by his words "a beautiful woman," realizing he meant her.

He gave a short laugh at her indecipherable response and leaned against the wall, pulling Tiffany towards him. Tiffany resisted. She felt her awkwardness retreating and her strength roaring back. She sensed danger in his lopsided smile that now resembled a sneer, the dimple in retreat.

"Those are some nice bed clothes for the middle of the day. Very sexy." He tightened his grip on her hand, rubbing the silken material with his free hand. "I think we can come to some mutually agreeable arrangement for today and the future."

Faster than she realized he could move, he pulled her to him and they shuffled her toward the door leading to her office. He opened it and made her go with him into the room without looking around, keeping his gaze on her. "Your eyes are quite a feast," he said gaily.

She could not speak nor look away. His face was so close to hers. Tiffany wondered if he was going to kiss her. Her thoughts snapped to more immediate concerns. He would see. He would see. She resisted, but he had pinned her arms. He was just too strong for her to break the hold, and yet, a part of her still wanted him, to experience him. She had yearned for so long, but not in here, not now.

He picked her up in one swift movement, and then turned, facing the large room with the partitioned office area. With his arms locked around her, she saw his expression change.

"What in tarnation?"

Struggling to get free, she brushed a column of cans. They tumbled down, then another column, and another. Hundreds of cans clanged down. He released her and backed out of the room. He backed into the dining room table and sat down awkwardly on a chair. She wanted to scream at him for ruining the moment, while she was trying to stop the avalanche of cans. She grunted. "Years of careful stacking now ruined by you." She faced him. The shocked look on his face alternated between the door to the room and her. Her anger rose as she calculated what she had lost and would lose. He stood, then stammered, "I'll let the lawyers handle this...situation." As he stumbled to exit the apartment, she cut in front of him. He circled around her trying to reach the door. Before he could unlatch the lock, her frying pan met his head.

#

Tiffany sensed his awakening and pumped harder. He moaned. He sweated. At times, she couldn't tell if he was crying or enjoying himself. Yet, through it all, his erection remained strong until both of them were satisfied. In that moment and space, she didn't care if it was love or lust. It was what it was. She lay down on his warm body, listening to the rapid beating of his heart. She had been right to gag and blindfold him. She knew that tying him to the four posts of the bed was wrong, but it was the right thing to do for now. She had to demonstrate her affection for him. She had to show what she could do for him. She had to make him understand that she was worthy of his seed and of her love. She cooled off, and then showered for the second time that day. That was something new too, and delightful in context.

She liked her outfit so much, she put it back on. When she returned to her office, she rebuilt the columns of cans without talking. It took a few hours. When finished, it was dark out. She closed the blinds. After struggling earlier, her new boyfriend had been quiet for some time. She imagined he probably had to do number 1 or number 2, but was unsure how to go about it. "Bed pan?" she said aloud. He seemed to agree. It took some maneuvering, but after accomplishing her mission, she slipped out of her pajamas. Flaccid at first, his manhood stood at attention after some encouragement from her. She mounted him and enjoyed herself thoroughly while bemoaning all the years wasted not being able to explore this aspect of life. Her father had ruined the best years of her life. She cried as much for her past as with her growing excitement. She still hated him and her mother. Him, for what he had done, and her, for allowing him to do so. They had destroyed her youthful awakening and derailed her future happiness. She deserved this man's love for so many reasons. She knew she could make him happy.

Her boyfriend resisted again at first, but then seemed thrilled by her efforts. She climaxed, and then, repeated. "I've read about this," she said, her voice quivering. "Oh, my!" she cooed. After a time, they trailed off. She was exhausted and he was spent. "This is what you really came for, isn't it? No one wants to buy my apartment. No one told you about me, but you did see me. You were spying all the time. I knew I wasn't being paranoid. You wanted me. I am pretty."

His initial delay in responding to her allegations angered her, but he eventually nodded. She kissed him on the cheek and then whispered in his ear, "Thank you." She swore she felt life growing inside of her already.

She undid the blindfold and then wished she hadn't. The anger in his eyes was palpable. His focus darted from her to the office filled with stacked cans and back to the other bed. He did it repeatedly, furrowing his brow deeper each time.

"You don't love me," she said. Disappointed, she bowed her head and her long flowing hair blanketed his face. "Something will need to be done about that."

Michael's hand grabbed Tiffany by the back of the neck and yanked her head, slamming it against the bed's railing. She caught a glimpse of the slender rope. He must have rubbed it back and forth for hours to cut it. He attempted to slam her head again, but she resisted, and then pounded him in the gut with one fist while prying his fingers from the hold he had on her neck and hair. "Mom. Dad. Help me." The stalemate continued until she hit him in the mouth. He gurgled, then seemed to be on the verge of passing out. He released his hold.

She sprinted to the kitchen. When she returned, he nearly had his other hand free. She plunged the carving knife into his chest. He shuddered a few times before rolling his eyes in the direction of the other bed and releasing a final breath.

She was exhausted, but before she showed up to work the next morning, she cleaned up the mess in the bedroom and made sure he was wrapped in cellophane and positioned between her parents on the other bed.

~~~~~

ACKNOWLEDGEMENTS

This is an incomplete list of those who have critiqued, complained, remarked, inspired, read, edited, guffawed, and otherwise shaped these short stories. Sometimes it is does take a village to rein in the idiot.

G. K. Adams, Ignatius Aloysius, Angel Alvarez, Daniel Aughey, Pat Bell, Michael Baird, Jeannette de Beauvoir, Peter Bernhardt, Tracy Bird, Ted Bookyak, Carrie Bylina, Jan Campana Melissa Ryan Chipman, Monica Di Santi, Albert Ervine, Margaret Frey, Charles Jackson, Mel Jacob, Patricia L. Johnson, Glen Jones, Carol Kean, Ida Kotyuk, Marianne Kulick, Robert J. Lewis, Jr., KW McCabe, Ashley Memory, Pauline Micciche, Patrick Murphy, Edith Parzefall, Paul Pekin, Eric Peterson, Judith Queaempts, Elias Rodriguez, Shelia Rudesil, Behlor Santi, Wayne Scheer, Fish Splash, Sydney, Barbara Taylor, Shannon Turner, Silvia Villalobos, Ron Voigts, and Bob White.

Also, the members of these fine organizations who I may have overlooked but who have, over the past ten years, contributed to these stories. My recordkeeping is not what it should be.

Internet Writing Workshop, Revolving Door Book Club, Hell's Angels, Writer's Retreat Workshop graduates, Writers Morning Out.

~~~~~

ABOUT THE AUTHOR

Rick Bylina lives with his wife, Carrie, and 20-year-old cockatiel, Sydney, near Apex, North Carolina. Ongoing corporate downsizing convinced him to tap into his passion. He scribed any crazy idea that crossed his mind. After gaining discipline, he wrote his debut mystery novel, *ONE PROMISE TOO MANY*, the first in a series, featuring Detective Roger Stark. Next was, *A MATTER OF FAITH*. *ALL OF OUR SECRETS* is his third novel. A collection of short stories, *BATHROOM READING: Short Stories for Short Visits* is in your hands, or should be. Writing happens spontaneously between housework, gardening, cooking, and wrestling alligators.

~~~~~

ABOUT SYDNEY

Sydney was born in a cardboard box in North Raleigh, North Carolina on March 17, 1992. He'll tell you he's from Australia, but he can never seem to find it on the globe. We adopted him six weeks later. He's extremely friendly unless you are a female child. We think he senses the exuberant energy. Favorite foods are mashed potatoes, turkey, spaghetti, rice, Cheerios, and banana. He hates fingers pointed at his face, mice, and bugs. He's always up for a rousing game of knocking the dishtowel off the countertop. His favorite place to be is on Rick's knee while he writes. He's working on his first novel, "Places I've Flown to in My Dreams".

Sydney says, "Peek-a-boo!"

CONNECTING WITH THE AUTHOR

Twitter: https://twitter.com/RickBylina

Facebook: https://www.facebook.com/rick.bylina

My blog: http://rickbylina.blogspot.com/

LinkedIn: www.linkedin.com/profile/rickbylina

Email: anilyb@earthlink.net

~~~~~

Made in the USA
Lexington, KY
24 November 2012